Praise for *New York Times* bestselling author Alexandra Ivy and her *Guardians of Eternity* series!

DARKNESS UNLEASHED

"*Darkness Unleashed* is oh, so hot and wonderfully dangerous. I can't wait for the next installment!"
Gena Showalter, *New York Times* bestselling author

"*Darkness Unleashed* is a fun ride! Jagr is YUMMY!"
Jade Lee, *USA Today* bestselling author

DARKNESS REVEALED

"A darkly erotic adventure with a vampire hero who can bite me anytime! Readers will adore Cezar's deliciously romantic craving for feisty, idealistic Anna Randal."
Angela Knight, *New York Times* bestselling author

DARKNESS EVERLASTING

"Ivy again provides vast quantities of adventure, danger and sizzling passion, ensuring her place on the list of rising paranormal stars."
Romantic Times

EMBRACE THE DARKNESS

"Delivers plenty of atmosphere and hot-blooded seduction."
Publishers Weekly

"Ivy creates such vivid and complex characters, their emotional struggles feel real even though their exploits are supernatural. A true gift to the genre."
Romantic Times (Top Pick!)

WHEN DARKNESS COMES

"Hot author Ivy bursts into the paranormal scene and her vampire trilogy launch is not to be missed. A big plus in this novel are the excellent characters, which help build a believable world with paranormal elements and highly passionate romance. Vivid secondary characters help set the stage and anticipation level for further chapters. Ivy is definitely an author with huge potential in the paranormal genre."
Romantic Times (Top Pick!)

Books by Alexandra Ivy

WHEN DARKNESS COMES

EMBRACE THE DARKNESS

DARKNESS EVERLASTING

DARKNESS REVEALED

DARKNESS UNLEASHED

BEYOND THE DARKNESS

DEVOURED BY DARKNESS

BOUND BY DARKNESS

MY LORD VAMPIRE

And don't miss these Guardians of Eternity novellas

TAKEN BY DARKNESS in YOURS FOR ETERNITY

DARKNESS ETERNAL in SUPERNATURAL

WHERE DARKNESS LIVES in
THE REAL WEREWIVES OF VAMPIRE COUNTY

My Lord Vampire

IMMORTAL ROGUES

ALEXANDRA IVY

ZEBRA BOOKS
KENSINGTON PUBLISHING CORP.

ZEBRA BOOKS are published by

Kensington Publishing Corp.
119 West 40th Street
New York, NY 10018

ISBN-13: 978-1-61793-672-2

Printed in the United States of America

For Chance and Alexander,
my very own vampires

Prologue
Behind the Veil

Gideon glided through the vaulted marble corridors of the Great Hall. A thick hush filled the ancient air, stirred only by the occasional rush of a scurrying servant. It was an unnatural silence. As a rule the spiderweb of corridors were filled with vampires seeking entrance to the vast library or attending the endless debates in one of the antechambers. There was no greater duty for a vampire than searching for knowledge. It was an insatiable thirst, and the only true desire that had remained since they had left the mortal plane to exist behind the Veil.

It had been nearly two hundred years since the great vampire Nefri had used the Medallion to create the Veil. Two hundred years of serenity and utter peace.

They had left behind the chaos and compulsive passions of the mortal world. They had also left behind the bloodlust that had made vampires as savage and brutal as the humans they preyed upon.

Since then it had been a time of immeasurable greatness for the Immortal Ones. Without the passions and hungers of the flesh they had reached a superior society that transcended any loss of powers they had suffered. Shape-shifting and mist walking that came only from the drinking of human blood were talents needed only for those who hunted.

And vampires no longer hunted.

Or they had not until this morning, Gideon sternly corrected.

A frown marred the fiercely elegant features as he considered the shocking revelations the Great Council had bestowed upon him.

It was near sacrilege to consider the notion that there would be traitors among the vampires. It was simply assumed that they had evolved far beyond petty jealousy and the lust for power. Surely such superior beings would be above the flaws of mere mortals?

Unfortunately there was no means of denying the startling truth that three powerful vampires had recently slipped through the Veil to the world of men. Or that they intended to battle for control of the Medallion.

A chill threatened to pierce the magnificent calm that had shrouded about Gideon for two centuries.

The traitors could not be allowed to gain command of the ancient artifact. With such raw power they could do untold damage.

Including ripping the Veil to shreds and challenging the authority of the Great Council itself.

The chaos that would ensue did not bear imagining, Gideon acknowledged with cold determination.

Thank blessed Nefri that she had possessed the sense to realize the impending danger and had managed to separate the Medallion. She had then given the pieces to three maidens who had no notion of the power they held.

The desperate measure had momentarily protected the Medallion from the clutches of the renegades, but it would only be a matter of time before they went in search of the maidens.

Which was precisely why he had been summoned to the Great Hall.

Almost reluctantly he glanced down at the dagger he held in his long, pale fingers. In the soft light it appeared nondescript with a smooth ivory handle. Only the trained eye of a vampire could detect the unmistakable shimmer of magic that rippled over the steel blade.

His frown deepened.

The mere thought of killing another vampire was utterly repellant. It was perhaps the greatest of sins. He would as soon sacrifice himself. But he had his commands.

He, Lucien and Sebastian were commanded to travel through the Veil and protect the maidens who unwittingly held the Medallion.

By any means necessary.

His fingers clenched about the dagger.

Any means.

Chapter I

Simone, Lady Gilbert, allowed a satisfied smile to curve her lips.

The stuccoed town house in the southern end of Park Lane was a Palladian masterpiece. Although not the largest home in London it was undoubtedly one of the most elegant with its wide marble foyer and double staircase that led to a long picture gallery. There was a clever balcony that overlooked the park that had been transformed into a conservatory and a formal drawing room with a great deal of gilding and masterpieces from Flemish artists. As the crowning glory the ballroom held a hint of Versailles with surrounding mirrors, heavy chandeliers and French furnishings.

It was a home fit for a Countess.

And it was all hers.

The smug satisfaction only deepened as Simone allowed her emerald green gaze to wander over the numerous guests who filled the crimson and gold parlor. Politicians, poets, scholars and aristocrats mingled together in happy harmony. Her salons were famous for assembling only the brightest, most intellectual of London's society, and invitations were battled over more fiercely than any voucher to Almack's. In fact, she had been forced to hire a large butler who had one time been a champion in the boxing ring to guard her door from those who would force their way into her home. It appeared that anyone who wished to be considered all the rage had to make an appearance at a party hosted by the "Wicked Temptress."

Not bad for a woman who had spent the past twenty-three years isolated in a remote part of Devonshire and who had never thought to enter society, let alone become the undoubted leader.

"Another stunning success, my temptress," a low, seductive voice whispered close to her ear.

Simone gave a last glance to ensure all was well before turning to greet the short, portly gentleman who was regarding her like a prospective morsel he longed to have a taste of.

"Good evening, Lord Braceton," she murmured, tilting her head so that her long, shimmering blond hair tumbled over her shoulders left bare by her dark emerald gown. She heard the older gentleman suck in a breath and she hid a satisfied smile. Since her arrival in London she had discovered her beauty was a potent weapon that could not be underestimated. Along with a bold, determined style and cunning elusiveness she had managed to create precisely the image best to tantalize the jaded members of town. "I trust you are enjoying your evening?"

An intelligence that had led him to be one of the most dangerous and powerful politicians in the House of Lords sparkled in his blue eyes.

"As well as could be expected considering I would prefer to damn this lot of insufferable bores to the netherworld so that we could be alone."

"Bores?" She arched a golden brow. "I will have you know that I carefully chose each guest for their ability to charm, tantalize or entertain me."

"Indeed?" The gentleman stepped closer, his gaze sweeping hungrily over her slender curves. "And why was I chosen, my dear? To tantalize, I hope."

"Comic relief, of course," she smoothly parried.

He stiffened briefly at the insult, then a grudging smile curved his thick lips.

"Such cruelty from such beauty," he mourned softly. "Tell me what I must do to win that cold heart of yours."

Simone gently waved her ivory-handled fan, her gaze returning to study the guests that moved through the room.

"I do not believe it is my heart you seek to win, my lord."

"Perhaps not." He gave a chuckle. "A fortunate thing considering that most among society do not believe that you possess the finer sensibilities. The more romantic, of course, presume that you buried your ability to love with your dear, departed husband. The more envious claim you were born heartless."

It was a testament to her sheer strength of will that Simone managed to appear languidly unconcerned at the charge. She briefly wondered what this gentleman would say if she revealed that she had felt nothing but contempt for Lord Gilbert, and that it had been her own sister who had destroyed her youthful heart.

"Ah, and what do you believe?" she drawled with supreme unconcern.

Lord Braceton shifted closer, risking one of Simone's notorious flayings.

"I believe you are simply awaiting the proper gentleman to awaken your slumbering emotions. No matter how cold and aloof you might wish to appear you cannot completely disguise the heat that shimmers in your blood. It is why we poor sods continue to flutter about you like moths drawn to the flame. No matter how often you singe our battered pride we simply cannot resist temptation."

Simone deliberately shifted away from the portly form. Although she was quite willing to indulge in a bit of flirtation, she was always careful to ensure that none of her admirers managed to convince themselves that she would be willing to be seduced.

"How very dramatic you are on this evening intended for frivolous pleasure," she lightly chastised, her emerald eyes darkening with a hint of warning. "The price no doubt of possessing a flamboyant and highly temperamental actress as your current lover."

There was a startled silence at Simone's daring words before his lordship tilted back his head to laugh with rich enjoyment.

"A meaningless distraction until the object of my desire agrees to halt tormenting me," he assured her with a twinkling gaze.

Simone gave a shake of her head at his persistence. "Really, my lord . . ." She began only to tense as she felt an odd prickle race over her skin.

A chill inched down her spine as Simone realized that someone from across the room was watching her. Watching her with such intensity that she could physically feel the relentless gaze as it made a lazy survey of her slender form.

It was a sensation she had never experienced before, and she discovered that there was something unnervingly intimate in the warm heat gliding over her skin.

Thrusting aside the strange sense of unease, Simone forced herself to turn and discover the source of that bothersome gaze.

It took a moment to discover the tall gentleman standing alone in a distant corner, but when she at last caught sight of him, her heart stuttered to a sudden halt.

Although he was properly attired in a black coat, pantaloons and a crisply tied cravat, he bore no resemblance to the other gentlemen that lounged about the room.

Well over six feet there was a raw, elegant power in his lean form that Simone could sense even at a distance. It was in the manner he leaned negligently against a marble column and in the arrogant tilt of his head. Her gaze narrowed as she studied the pale, finely chiseled features that were framed by his long, satin hair the shade of polished ebony.

His male beauty was enough to steal her breath.

Against her will she found herself lingering upon the aquiline nose, the high thrust of his cheekbones and sensuous curve of his lips. There was a compelling strength and unrelenting pride etched into those features that sent a rash of warning down her spine.

This was not a gentleman who could be toyed with and kept at a safe distance. He was a conqueror who would stride through the world and take what he desired.

Then, she lifted her head to meet the black, brooding gaze and her knees nearly gave way.

There was a searing heat in those eyes that flared across the room and swept through her body. Simone reeled in startled bewilderment as she was helplessly trapped by that dark regard.

Suddenly she understood precisely how a fly felt when it stumbled into the web of a spider.

"Dear heavens," she whispered softly.

At last realizing that he had lost her attention, Lord Braceton turned to follow her gaze.

"What?"

"Who is that gentleman?" she demanded as she struggled to regain command of her shattered composure.

The older man heaved a heavy sigh. "Mr. Gideon Ravel. He just arrived in London with his two cousins from the Continent. Seems he's related to some aristocratic family or other. They made quite a stir when they appeared at the Croswell's ball last week."

A shiver raced through her. She could imagine that this man would make a stir wherever he might be. Even now her guests were glancing in the stranger's direction and whispering in low voices. Mr. Ravel remained splendidly unconcerned at the obvious interest in his arrival as he continued to regard her with that unwavering gaze.

Simone unconsciously squared her shoulders as she realized that she was staring at the man like a half-wit.

This was her home.

And no one entered it without her invitation.

No one.

"How the devil did he manage to get past Bartson?" she gritted in annoyance.

At her side Lord Braceton gave a shrug. "Perhaps he came with one of your other guests."

"Impossible. Only those with invitations are allowed to enter. Excuse me."

Without awaiting her companion's response, Simone swept through the mingling crowd toward the gentleman watching her with that faintly mocking smile. At the same moment an elderly gentleman stepped to join the stranger, attempting to claim his attention, although that black gaze remained firmly trained upon her flushed countenance.

A rather cowardly urge to wait until he was once again alone swept through Simone before she was swiftly thrusting it aside.

What the blazes was wrong with her? She was no longer a cowering maiden who cringed at the mere hint of a threat. After the death of her sister she had refused to be frightened of anyone ever again.

Regardless if that anyone happened to be a towering, black-haired devil with eyes of midnight.

Keeping that thought firmly in the forefront of her mind, Simone swept to a halt directly in front of the intruder, her smile intact as the elderly gentleman next to him turned to regard her with a mild lift of his brows.

"Good evening, Lord Tydale," she murmured, her gaze never wavering from the midnight eyes.

Simone discovered her throat dangerously dry as she felt the smoldering power of the stranger reach out to wrap about her. Botheration. She had never encountered anyone who unsettled her in such a fashion. The realization only sharpened her temper.

"Ah, our charming hostess." Tydale performed a respectable bow, politely ignoring the fact that his two companions were far too consumed with one another to bother glancing in his direction. "My dear, you are appearing as devilishly delectable as always. You really must confess the name of your modiste. It is unconscionable that the other ladies in the Ton must always pale in comparison."

Simone's smile thinned. No one but her servants knew that she designed and stitched her own gowns. Not only because she truly enjoyed creating the lovely dresses, but because she could not possibly allow a modiste to catch a glimpse of her in a mere shift. Her charade would be over as swiftly as it had begun.

"That is entirely the point of keeping her name secret," she forced herself to say in light tones.

"So wicked," the elderly gentleman chided.

"I do not believe I have been introduced to your companion."

"Actually I am not at all certain I wish to oblige you with an introduction, Simone," Lord Tydale teased, clearly sensing the silent battle of wills that hung heavy in the air. "After only a week this gentleman has managed to wreak havoc among the fairer sex. I daresay there is not a maiden in London who has not tossed her heart at his feet."

She slowly arched her brows as she regarded Mr. Ravel. "Since I have never been foolish enough to toss my heart at any gentleman's feet, I believe you are safe in making the introduction."

Tydale heaved a resigned sigh. "Oh, very well, but do not say I did not attempt to warn you of his dastardly charm. Lady Gilbert, may I make you known to Mr. Ravel?"

Fiercely aware of that haughty black stare, Simone sank into a shallow curtsy.

"Mr. Ravel."

His bow was even more brief. "Lady Gilbert."

Simone gritted her teeth. "Lord Tydale, would you be kind enough to procure me a glass of champagne?"

There was a moment's pause before the older man gave a reluctant grimace. "But of course. I shall return."

Lord Tydale grudgingly turned to move away, and Mr. Ravel boldly flicked his gaze over her slender form.

"Do all gentlemen leap to your commands so swiftly, Lady Gilbert?"

Simone was startled by the soft, seductively dark tones. There was a faint trace of an accent but it oddly only made his voice more pleasing.

She gave an unwitting shake of her head, attempting to clear her suddenly thick thoughts.

There was something . . . something drawing her into a strange sense of lethargy that made it difficult to think of anything beyond the tempting beauty of his ebony eyes.

She swayed forward, nearly lost in the darkness before she was belatedly grasping her elusive anger and gathering it about her like a tattered shroud. She tilted her chin upward.

"Those who wish to please me," she said in an admirably steady voice.

Something that might have been surprise rippled over the pale, elegant features before Mr. Ravel allowed his lips to curl upward.

"Ah, a woman who demands obedience," he mocked. "Tell me, my dear, do you not find admirers with no will of their own rather tedious? There are, after all, faithful hounds if you wish utter submission. A gentleman of genuine strength could provide a great deal more. Anything you could desire."

Her irritation deepened. How dare he sneak into her home, blatantly stare at her as if she were a common tart and then treat her with such aloof amusement?

"I understand that you are relatively new to London."

He shrugged. "I arrived last week."

"From the Continent?"

"Yes."

She glared into the unearthly magnificence of his countenance. "Alone?"

"No. I have two cousins who traveled with me. They were unfortunately unable to join me this evening."

Her lips tightened at the implication that his cousins would have been as arrogant as he in thrusting themselves into a gathering where they were not invited.

"Are you visiting family?"

"No, I have a small commission to be discharged and then I shall return to my home."

"And where precisely is your home?" she persisted, refusing to be daunted by the cool haughtiness etched into his expression.

The pale slender fingers lifted to absently play with a diamond pin in the folds of his cravat. She discovered herself nearly hypnotized by the languid movement. He possessed the hands of an artist, she thought fuzzily. How would it feel to have those fingers stroking her overheated skin . . .

Simone shuddered in shock as she hastily thrust the renegade thought away.

"You are very inquisitive," he drawled in those smoky tones.

"Am I?" She forced herself to meet that disturbing gaze squarely. "Well, perhaps that is because I am unaccustomed to having strangers invade my home. I am very select in who receives an invitation."

"Ah." He remained supremely unconcerned at her insult. "A wise precaution, no doubt."

"I think so. It would not do to have a clever encroacher thrusting their way into society."

"An encroacher?" A chiseled ebony brow slowly lifted. "You do not believe anyone would possess the audacity to boldly enter society without the proper bloodlines?"

A near hysterical giggle rose to her throat before she sternly subdued it. What was the matter with her? She would give all away if she were not careful.

"Yes, I do."

The dark eyes seemed to narrow. "An interesting notion."

Realizing she was treading dangerous waters, Simone prepared to take a more direct approach. Clearly the gentleman could not be shamed by more subtle means.

"I believe, sir, you are being deliberately obtuse," she charged in low tones.

The thick brow inched higher. "Deliberately? Could it not be that I am merely unintentionally obtuse? After all, the proper bloodlines have never ensured intelligence."

Her teeth gritted. "How did you enter my home?"

"I assure you I did not materialize from thin air." He appeared amused by her rising irritation. "I walked through the front door as any proper guest would do."

"Impossible," Simone retorted, thinking of the large, barrel-chested Bartson. No matter how dangerous this man might be he could not have bested her servant without a very noisy struggle. "My butler would never have allowed anyone in without an invitation."

He offered an elegant shrug. "He was quite understanding when I revealed that I had only recently arrived in London. I assured him that had you known of my presence you most certainly would have desired me to attend your elegant gathering. We are, after all, destined to be quite intimately acquainted."

Intimately?

A feather of fear whispered through her heart.

He sounded so utterly confident. So sure of himself.

She gave a sharp shake of her head. "Bartson would never have believed such nonsense."

Those fingers stilled upon the diamond pin. "Why not? It is the simple truth."

Once again she felt that compelling force of him reach out to wrap about her. It was almost tangible and Simone battled to clear her foggy mind.

"I think you must be mad," she whispered with an unconscious frown.

Without warning the beautiful male features hardened and a glitter entered the black eyes.

"You have yet to know true madness," he informed her in low tones. "But you will. And very soon I fear."

She took an abrupt step backward, barely preventing herself from glancing about and ensuring that she was still surrounded by glittering guests.

She would not be frightened nor intimidated, she sternly reminded herself. Not again.

"Why are you here?"

Rather surprisingly he allowed his gaze to drift downward, lingering for a long moment upon the golden Medallion that she wore upon a slender chain. Oddly the metal seemed almost to warm as it lay between the curves of her breasts.

"To fulfill destiny, my dear Lady Gilbert. Soon enough you will be grateful for my presence."

She blinked at his mysterious words, her fingers unconsciously reaching up to grasp the Medallion in a tight grip.

"Highly doubtful," she forced herself to mutter. "I wish you to leave my home, sir."

There was a ripple of muscles as he straightened from the column and towered over her.

"Is that a command?"

"I . . . yes."

Their gazes locked and clashed before a chilled smile curved the sensuous lips.

"A word of warning, my dear. Unlike these gentlemen whom you regard as mere flunkies, you cannot command me, or seduce me to your will. We will play this game by my rules."

Simone did not need the warning. Everything about this remote, elegant stranger spoke of danger. She was not a fool.

"There is to be no game between us at all," she informed him in cold tones. "Indeed, I never intend to set eyes upon you again."

"A rather difficult task considering that I will be calling upon you tomorrow."

She stiffened at his audacity. What the devil did this man want from her?

"Do not dare," she warned, her emerald eyes flashing with fire. "You will be turned away at the door."

Indifferent to her anger, Mr. Ravel smoothly reached out to grasp her hand before she even realized his intent. Simone caught her breath as searing heat shivered over her gloveless fingers, her stomach clenching in the oddest manner. She was so startled by the unexpected sensations she did not even protest as he lowered his head and stroked his warm lips over the inner skin of her wrist. Her heart stuttered, nearly coming to a complete halt before abruptly racing out of control. His lips barely caressed her, yet she felt as if she had been branded by his touch.

Her eyes were wide and darkened with a traitorous awareness when he slowly lifted his head to sweep his midnight gaze over her flushed countenance.

"You underestimate my powers of persuasion. A dangerous fault," he murmured, allowing her hand to drop so that he could reach up to stroke the silky strands of her golden hair. "Wear your hair down again tomorrow. I find it quite enticing."

With her knees shaking and her blood far warmer than it should be, Simone gaped at him in outrage.

"Why you . . ." She began to stammer, only to realize there were not words to express her tumultuous emotions.

His smile widened. "Yes?"

Realizing that she had at last encountered a gentleman whom she could not tame to her satisfaction, Simone accepted that the only thing left was a dignified retreat. It was far too late to wish that she had simply ignored his unwelcome presence and maintained a cool disdain. Now she had to hope that his stay in London would be very brief indeed.

"Good night, Mr. Ravel," she retorted in tight tones. "I would say it has been a pleasure, but not even good manners can force such a lie to my lips."

His fingers drifted from her hair to lightly brush her cheek. "Perhaps it has not been a pleasure, but you will think of me tonight, my dear. Until tomorrow."

Simone did not wait for his elegant bow.

Feeling more uneasy than she had since the first days she had arrived alone and frightened in London, Simone turned on her heel and fled through the room.

Gideon slipped through the shadows of the garden with fluid ease. With his black cape rippling about his lean form he blended into darkness with silent ease. Not even the dog sleeping near the hedge took note as he drifted past and headed toward the mews.

Not far from where he walked the light and music spilled from Lady Gilbert's town house onto the neatly pruned roses. Barely aware of what he did, Gideon slowed and regarded the large house.

He was still adjusting to returning to the world of mortals.

It had not been an easy task.

His body felt heavy and plagued with the desires it had not experienced in two centuries. Hunger, passion, and overall the intoxicating scent of warm blood. Like an aphrodisiac it shrouded Gideon in temptation. So much power there for the taking. Heady, delicious power. He would be invincible, a seductive voice whispered deep in his heart. A vampire of old who walked through the night in mist and shadow, taking pleasure where he chose and drowning himself in the passions of his human flesh.

Gideon discovered himself trembling with the effort to control his suddenly raging emotions. He had underestimated the dark lure of lust. Power, passion and a primitive thirst to conquer warred with the cold command that was his birthright.

Gideon gave a sharp shake of his head. Through the windows of the town house he could make out the slender outline of Simone Gilbert.

Ah, now that was temptation, indeed.

Sweet temptation.

He gave a low snarl of annoyance.

He had not expected to find the maiden a beautiful minx with hair of spun gold and eyes that dared him to taste of her smoldering desire. Nor that he would react with such force to her enticing presence.

He had come to save his world from the traitors who would destroy it, he reminded himself with a stern chastisement. He could not afford to be distracted by the weakness of his flesh.

A hint of a frown marred his noble brow.

There were bound to be problems, he grimly conceded.

Simone had already revealed a stubborn, wary nature that was certain to revolt if he were to command her to obey his orders. And his subtle attempt at a Compulsion spell had been effectively blocked by the Medallion she wore about her neck. A difficulty he had not expected.

He would have to somehow convince her that she must accept his protection without revealing the true reason for her danger.

And at the same time keep a close guard on the renegades who would do whatever necessary to lay their hands upon that Medallion.

His lips twisted in a cold smile. He could only hope that Lucien and Sebastian were having better luck than he was.

Turning back toward the hedge Gideon continued his gliding path toward the back of the gardens.

Upon arriving in London he had first set about acquiring a home in Mayfair and suitable staff to ensure that he was readily accepted as a foreign noble with the sort of fortune that would buy him entrance to the Ton. After that had been the tedious task of meeting with a tailor and boot maker, as well as buying a proper carriage and horses.

Once he was certain that his image was well established he had swiftly made his way to the stews to discover a small army of street urchins who would act as his eyes and ears throughout town.

Foregoing the more brutal Inscrolling spells that would make humans faithful, but mindless, slaves to a vampire and even the lesser Compulsion spells, Gideon had chosen the simplest means of assuring their loyalty.

Bribery.

Now he silently slid behind the ragged youth that was crouched behind a rosebush. With uncanny swiftness the villain turned to confront him with a knife in his hand. Gideon was suitably impressed by the boy's ability to sense his presence. Such skill would serve him well.

"Hold, it is I," he said in low tones.

With a saucy grin the youth gave the knife a twirl before it disappeared into the grimy sleeve of his jacket.

"Guv."

"Have you noted anything unusual?"

The grin spread across the bony face. "A right fair number of those fancy guests have a queer interest in that tiny building." He jerked his head toward the shadowed gazebo that was obviously a perfect spot for seduction. "Been tramping in and out all evening."

A brief image of Simone floating down the path toward the gazebo where he would readily join her in rose-scented passion was fiercely thrust away. Sweet

Nefri, did the woman have magic of her own? Had she managed to bewitch him?

Cloaking himself in icy control, Gideon regarded his young servant with a glittering gaze.

"A straight answer if you please."

The lad dropped his false air of bravado and gave a somber nod. "Yes, sir. Seen a bloke slip through the garden and onto the terrace near an hour ago."

Gideon was on instant alert. "What did he look like?"

A shudder abruptly raced through the boy. "Difficult to say in the dark, but I do know he was tall and thin with a cape like yer own. Hair seemed a funny silver like, but it could be the moonlight."

"Tristan," he muttered, easily able to identify one of the renegades. A vampire with considerable power, he was more crafty than intelligent, and always brutal. He was also notoriously impatient. Gideon would have to consider how best to use that weakness to his own advantage. "He now knows that I am here."

"Beg pardon, sir, but he gave me a right queer feeling."

Gideon snapped his attention back to the youth standing before him. "You did not approach him, did you?"

"No." He gave a violent shake of his head. "I stayed right in the bushes as you said. Still . . . I shouldn't like to come up against him in a dark alley."

"It would be even worse than you could ever imagine," Gideon assured him in bleak tones. Were Tristan to discover that this boy was in his employ the vampire would take great delight in torturing him beyond all bearing. "You are to have nothing to do with him. Is that understood?"

The boy turned to spit upon the ground. "Couldn't pay me enough to tangle with that bugger. Makes me feel like the night me da locked me in a crypt for spilling his gin. Nasty business."

Gideon arched a brow at the youth's perception. "You possess a rare insight for a mere mort . . . boy," he smoothly corrected.

That crooked grin returned. "I live on the streets, guv. I would have been dead long ago if I couldn't smell trouble."

"I suppose so." Gideon straightened, knowing he still had a long night ahead of him searching for Tristan's lair. "You know what is to be done?"

The boy heaved a breath at his question. He had been forced to repeat the command over and over until Gideon was certain that he had it memorized.

"Two of us on duty at all times. If the lady leaves we are to follow at a safe distance. If we notice anything a bit off we are to fetch you at yer home."

"Anything," Gideon stressed in tones that rippled through the air. "Even if it appears harmless."

The lad gave a mocking salute. "Righto, guv."

Gideon briefly considered the boy then; realizing he had done all that was possible to keep Simone safe, he gave a smooth nod of his head.

"I shall meet with you again tomorrow."

Turning on his heel Gideon faded into the shadows. No one could see him halt one more time to glance toward the figure still outlined in front of the window before he was slipping through the mews and on the hunt for a silver-haired vampire.

Chapter 2

It had been a long, frustrating night for Gideon.

Upon more than one level, he reluctantly conceded as he moved up the steps to Simone's town house.

Not only had he failed to find any trace of Tristan as he had searched through the streets of London, he had been unable to banish the thought of a golden-haired beauty with eyes of emeralds.

Even when he had at last accepted the limitations of his physical form and briefly lay upon his bed, he had been haunted by the vision of her graceful features and enticing curves. Curves that he did not doubt would fit perfectly beneath him.

The very fact he could not dismiss her from his thoughts had Gideon leaving his bed and attiring himself in black coat and breeches.

He disliked the sense of being controlled by the sudden passions that plagued him, he acknowledged sourly. The sooner he could track down Tristan and convince him of the futility of his cause, the sooner he could return behind the Veil.

But first he had to call upon Simone and somehow establish a means of forcing her to obey him.

His lips thinned. He would rather face the bloodthirsty Tristan.

Reaching the top step, Gideon patiently waited as the door was pulled open by the pug-faced butler who regarded him with a challenging stare. There was little doubt that the poor servant had been severely chastised for allowing him to pass last night, and that he fully intended to halt him today.

He was visibly bristling with aggression.

Stepping past the servant into the foyer, Gideon handed the man his hat and gloves.

"Mr. Ravel to see Lady Gilbert," he stated smoothly.

The servant jutted out his chin. "Her ladyship is not at home."

Gideon waved a slender hand, silently speaking the powerful words that would ensure he was allowed to see the stubborn minx. He did not possess the time for such nonsense.

"I fear you must be mistaken," he said softly.

"No, I . . ." The servant faltered as his thoughts became tangled. "I mean, she does not wish to see you."

"She will see me."

There was a strained silence. "I was commanded not to let you in."

"Now I am commanding you to allow me to pass."

"I . . ."

"Move aside."

There was a brief struggle before the butler was giving an obedient nod of his head.

"Yes, of course."

Gideon smiled with cold satisfaction. "I will show myself in."

"Very well."

Knowing that it would be some time before the butler realized that he had once again failed his mistress, Gideon moved toward the steps and fluidly swept upward. He paused briefly upon the landing, using his senses to draw him toward a room at the end of the gallery. Even before opening the door he could feel the maiden's tension as it hummed through the air. Somehow the thought that she was as unnerved as he brought a sense of satisfaction.

Moving with unearthly silence Gideon opened the door and slid into the ivory and gilded room. For a moment he merely watched the woman as she paced across the carpet, appreciating the manner the brilliant sapphire gown drifted about her slender curves, and the play of the afternoon sunlight in the flowing golden curls. There was a vibrant spirit about her that called to the stirring passions deep within him.

With a stern warning at his tenuous restraint he cloaked himself in the cool arrogance that had once seemed so effortless.

He was a superior being with powers beyond the comprehensions of a mere mortal.

No mere maiden was going to disrupt his equanimity. Or at least he would never reveal such weakness.

"Good day, Lady Gilbert," he greeted in tones as smooth as black velvet.

He watched the slender body stiffen and her hands clench at her side before Simone slowly turned to regard him with wide, disbelieving eyes.

"You. How . . . ?" She bit off her words as she noted the expectant glint in his dark eyes. With an obvious effort she attempted to appear unconcerned by his sudden arrival. "What are you doing here?"

He waved a negligent hand, refusing to allow his gaze to linger on the translucent perfection of the satin skin revealed by the low bodice. Or to notice the musky scent of rosewater that filled the air.

"What any gentleman would be doing when he has been captivated by a beautiful woman," he retorted as he strolled toward the center of the room. "I have come to pay homage."

The emerald eyes flared but surprisingly she did not accept his calculated words with the ease he had hoped.

"Fah."

"Fah?"

"You are not captivated." Her expression was one of stubborn suspicion. "And you are not here to pay homage. I have had enough time to consider your odd arrival at my home last evening."

A ripple of impatience threatened his calm demeanor. There was an unmistakable air of challenge about her that threatened to touch his more primitive nature.

"Indeed?" He stepped closer, hoping to intimidate her by his mere presence. "And what have you concluded?"

She fiercely held her ground, although he did not miss the manner her fingers clutched at the folds of her skirt.

"That you are not whom you seem to be."

Gideon regarded her a moment in silence, quite certain that she could not possibly have guessed the truth. Humans never desired to believe that there were powers beyond their comprehension.

"You still believe me to be an encroacher?" he demanded with a lift of his brow. "Shall I cut myself to prove my blue blood?"

Her features tightened, but Gideon suddenly sensed there was more than irritation behind her prickly unease. Despite all her bluff and bravado there was an unmistakable scent of fear in the air. Not a fear of her physical being, he carefully concluded, but a fear that he could harm her in some elusive fashion.

"What do you seek from me?" she demanded in tones that were not quite steady. "Is it money?"

Gideon regarded her with an arrested expression. The fear was now nearly palpable in the air.

She thought he desired money from her?

Why?

"Interesting." He studied the guarded features that held enough stubborn pride to do a vampire proud. What could possibly force such a woman to harbor such anxiety? "You think I have come to blackmail you?"

A shiver raced through her stiff form but she faced him squarely.

"Have you?"

"I wonder what dark secret you possess," he murmured softly. "It must be dark indeed to fear blackmail."

Her gaze narrowed with impatience. "I am in no humor to play these absurd games, sir. What is it that you want?"

He briefly considered the wisdom of using her unwitting weapon to hold her in his power, before he was thrusting it aside. Perhaps he could force her to obey his commands, but he oddly disliked the notion of allowing her to believe he was a cowardly buffoon who would abuse her secrets for his own gain.

What he desired was her trust, he realized with a flare of surprise.

"It is really quite simple," he informed her in silky tones. "I have come to protect you."

"Protect me?" Her golden brows pleated in a disbelieving frown. "That is ridiculous. I need no protection."

Foolish chit.

He briefly thought of Tristan standing upon the terrace last evening. With a single word he could have cloaked himself in mist and entered her home. She would have been dead before she ever realized she was in danger. Only the fact that she possessed the Medallion had thus far saved her. The renegade could not lure her with a spell, nor simply kill her. The Medallion had been bonded to her with a Soul Weave. Unless she gave it freely it could not be taken.

"That is because you do not yet realize your danger," he informed darkly.

"Danger from whom?"

"That is all I am willing to tell you."

"This is absurd." She folded her arms about her waist, unconsciously making the full curve of her bosom all the more visible. Gideon could almost taste the sweet heat of her skin. "I am not about to allow some arrogant stranger to thrust his way into my home under the pretext of a mythical danger you will not even reveal."

He gazed down the length of his thin nose. "Actually you have little choice in the matter."

The absolute authority in his tone made a tiny muscle in her jaw pulse. "I was right last night. You are mad."

Gideon shrugged, not about to indulge her in a futile argument. Protecting the Medallion was his entire purpose in being within the world of mortals. He would do whatever necessary.

Stepping close enough to be bathed in her rose scent, he allowed his gaze to lower toward the shimmering golden Medallion that lay against her white skin.

Although disguised as a simple amulet, his sensitive gaze could easily discern the power that pulsed within. He felt a small tingle of awe at the tangible symbol of Nefri and her glory.

"Tell me, Lady Gilbert, where did you buy that unusual necklace?"

She blinked in bewilderment at his sudden shift in conversation. "What?"

"It is a most interesting design."

Her lips thinned at his obvious ploy. "We were discussing your unwelcome presence in my home, not my necklace."

"You have a reason not to discuss the necklace?" he challenged smoothly. "You perhaps stole it?"

Predictably she bristled at his words. "Certainly not. If you must know it was given to me by an old gypsy."

He wondered what she would do if he were to tell her that it was a priceless relic that possessed untold power. And that the old gypsy had been the mightiest of all vampires.

No doubt she would truly label him mad.

Or run into the streets screaming with fear.

"That would explain the inscription," he murmured instead.

"You know what it means?" she said in surprise.

Unable to resist temptation Gideon lifted his hand to grasp the Medallion in his fingers.

Whether the temptation was to feel the shimmering power within the amulet or to have an excuse to allow his fingers to rest against the pearly softness of her skin he did not bother to ponder.

"'Those who search for peace have already discovered wisdom,'" he quoted in low tones.

"Oh," she breathed, her heart beating frantically at the light touch of his fingers.

"Did this gypsy tell you anything of this amulet?"

"Only some foolishness about never removing it at the risk of a terrible curse and that it can never be stolen, only freely given to another. The usual gypsy nonsense."

His eyes bored deep within her own, willing her to comprehend just how dangerous it would be to remove the Medallion.

"I would not dismiss her words so swiftly."

"I . . . surely you do not ask me to believe in curses?" she demanded, but without the bluster she had managed before.

"I ask you to believe that there are mysteries in the world that are not easily explained. Mysteries that defy logic."

"Mysteries such as you?" she charged.

"Yes."

He could not prevent the faint smile that suddenly curved his lips, nor the fingers that loosened their hold upon the amulet to softly explore the skin that was driving him to distraction. His breath caught as he skimmed the warm silkiness that he had not felt in two centuries.

Dark passions once again stirred within him, making the air feel as thick as honey. This woman possessed something . . . something that he had never before experienced. It threatened to unloosen the lust that smoldered deep within him.

His heart slowed as he watched his fingers travel over the sensuous curve of her breast, a building need to brand her as his own hardening his body.

He reached the edge of the bodice before she at last sucked in a sharp breath and gave a shake of her head.

"No. Please do not do that," she whispered in uneven tones.

It was the very fact he could feel the desire pulsing through her blood that at last brought him to his senses.

This was not a part of his plan, he reminded himself coldly. And whatever the pleasure it might provide it would only add complications to a very dangerous situation.

Still he could not deny that there was something to be said for encouraging her desire, a renegade voice whispered in the back of his mind.

She was too independent to meekly submit to another's commands, and too stubborn to accept that he might know what was best for her. Perhaps he could subdue her through her own devilish pride.

He had already witnessed the manner she used her beauty as a weapon over weak-willed men. And how indifferent she was to her ability to arouse their desires. It would not be easy for her to accept she might actually feel passion for a gentleman who was indifferent to her potent charms.

Surely such a woman would do whatever necessary to prove that she was irresistible?

Including putting aside her distrust in an effort to lure him into her web. Which would allow him to remain close enough to protect her.

A logical plan. As long as he kept his own passions locked deep within him.

Glancing into the wide emerald eyes, he lifted one dark brow.

"What is the matter? You do not need to be ashamed of your skin. It is as smooth as heated cream. Quite delectable, in fact."

"I do not want you to touch me," she forced herself to mutter.

He gave a low, throaty laugh. "Is that why you shiver beneath my fingers? Why your blood races?"

A sudden flush spread beneath her cheeks as she took an abrupt step backward.

"Why you arrogant . . . worm," she gritted in embarrassment.

He folded his arms over his chest. "There is nothing arrogant in my realization that you desire me."

She visibly tensed as she regarded him in frustration. It was obvious she was unaccustomed to encountering gentlemen who did not crawl upon their knees to please her.

He allowed his smile to widen.

"I was not the one to pursue you to your home, nor to . . . to fondle you," she spat out.

"I was merely seeking to discover if your skin is as soft as it appears."

The emerald eyes narrowed in a dangerous manner. "Mere curiosity?"

Thankful that she could not possibly know that his fingers still tingled with pleasure, nor that the demons still raged within him, Gideon offered a faint shrug.

"Yes."

"And you have no intention of attempting to seduce me?"

"No intention whatsoever," he assured her softly.

Momentarily caught off guard she frowned at him in confusion. Gideon briefly wondered if anyone had ever sought her out without a selfish motive. She seemed far too cynical for one so young.

"Fah," she at last breathed. "You are no different than any other man."

"Oh, I think you will discover I am quite, quite different than most gentlemen," he retorted, assuring himself that he did not feel a pang of remorse that he was using this maiden as everyone else seemingly did. Such weakness belonged to humans, not vampires. "I am sorry if you are disappointed. Perhaps during another time and in another place I might have satisfied your passions."

She gasped with sudden fury. "I . . ."

He moved so swiftly she was unable to react before he had swooped his head downward and gently pressed his lips to her own. Sparks flared as he briefly drank of her soft temptation, the scent of roses and warm blood clouding his mind before he was pulling back.

A shudder raced through him as he battled to regain control of his own fervor.

He had tested his restraint enough for now, he acknowledged with a pang of unease at the realization. It was time to return to his hunt.

"I have important matters that demand my attention," he informed her with an elegant bow. "Do not concern yourself, however, I shall soon return."

Pressing a hand to her lips she remained silent as he turned and crossed the room. It was not until he had at last reached the door that she regained command of herself.

"Despicable cad."

* * *

For the first time since arriving in London, Simone considered ignoring the numerous invitations that lay upon her dressing table and remaining quietly at home.

Even after several hours she was still brewing with anger at Mr. Gideon Ravel.

Never, never had she ever encountered such an aggravating man. Not only thrusting his way into her home, despite her long lecture to Bartson, but then giving her some absurd story of needing to protect her. As if she would need the assistance of an arrogant stranger who was clearly mad.

It was all utterly ridiculous.

Almost as ridiculous as the knowledge that his touch had deeply affected her.

Botheration. She had nearly swooned when his fingers had stroked so lightly over her. And then that kiss . . .

The heady sensations that had raced through her had stolen every rational thought and made her behave as foolishly as the most thick-skulled twit. Not even his humiliating declaration that he was not about to seduce her had managed to deaden the heated excitement that swirled through her body.

At least he had not seemed intent upon blackmail as she had first feared, she had tried to reassure herself. That thought had kept her awake long into the night. She could never afford to forget that her entire world could be destroyed in a single moment.

Spending the day pacing the floor of her bedchamber,

Simone had at last gathered her courage and attired herself in a glittering yellow gown.

She would not cower in her home because of Mr. Gideon Ravel, or any other man, she had told herself sternly. He might have bested her today, but the battle was far from over. She would teach him that she was no woman to trifle with.

Keeping that thought firmly in mind she had called for her carriage and arrived at the theater where she was to join a small, select party. She did not think to meet Mr. Ravel there, but she hoped that he would at least hear she had been in attendance with her usual serene composure.

Her determination briefly faltered as she entered the theater and was swiftly joined by a tall, gaunt-faced gentleman attired in a formal coat and knee breeches. Simone stiffened with displeasure as he glided close beside her, his long silver hair pulled into a queue at his neck.

She had no reasonable excuse for disliking Mr. Soltern. In truth he had been quite charming on the few occasions that their paths had crossed. But while he was always polite there was something about the gray, lifeless eyes that sent a chill over her skin.

Unconsciously she pulled away from his tall frame, her nose twitching at the vague, unpleasant scent of cold steel that seemed to shroud about him.

Perhaps noting her instinctive withdrawal, the gentleman bared his large teeth in what was no doubt intended as a smile.

"Ah, my fair angel. How fortunate I am to have crossed your path."

"Thank you, Mr. Soltern," she forced herself to say in pleasant tones.

"Tristan, my dear," he chided softly, waving the ebony cane that he held in a thin, bony hand. "I presume you have also been summoned to join Lord Stonewall in his box?"

She swallowed the instinctive denial. She could not simply turn and leave the theater just because she discovered this man was to be a part of her party. Such an insult might very well make him an enemy. And she possessed an uncanny sense that he would be a very dangerous foe.

"Yes, a tedious task, I fear. You need not bother to escort me."

"A task is never tedious in your charming company, Simone," he said with an unwelcome air of intimacy. "Indeed, I would be content to walk at your side for an eternity."

Simone shuddered in horror at the mere thought. "Very pretty, sir."

A silence fell as they climbed the wide stairs, then with a sideways glance Tristan gently cleared his throat.

"I understand that you had a rather unexpected guest at your salon last evening."

Simone stiffened before she could prevent the betraying motion. Damn the incessant tattlers. She did not like the thought of London gossiping about Mr. Ravel and their obvious confrontation.

"Did I?"

"A Mr. Ravel," he prompted her.

She kept her expression smoothly unconcerned. She certainly had no intention of adding to any speculation.

"Yes, now that you mention it, he did attend."

"He is an acquaintance of yours?"

"Of sorts," she readily lied, reluctantly turning to meet that dead gaze. "Why do you ask?"

He paused before lifting a thin shoulder. "I am merely concerned for your welfare."

Simone frowned at his words. This was the second occasion she had been warned that she was somehow in danger. A chill trickled down her spine.

"Concerned?"

"I have known Mr. Ravel for countless years and unfortunately I must confess that he is utterly untrustworthy."

Her expression became cool at the rapier edge in his voice. It was obvious he possessed a deep dislike for Mr. Ravel. And that he hoped to sway her own opinion.

Regardless of the fact she had devoted most of the day to cursing Gideon she was not about to be blindly informed of whom she could or could not trust. Certainly not by a man who made her skin crawl.

"In what manner?" she retorted in tones that should have warned the most obtuse she was displeased.

"He rarely speaks the truth and always possesses a hidden motive when offering his friendship. Especially in regards to beautiful and wealthy women."

"He is a fortune hunter?"

He heaved a sigh that hissed oddly through his teeth. "I am sad to say he is, indeed."

Simone firmly turned to regard the landing crowded with elegant guests. If Mr. Ravel were a fortune hunter, he would be far from the first to have attempted to lure her. She had been a target since arriving in London.

"I have no fear of being seduced out of my fortune, Mr. Soltern. I am no innocent chit who futilely clings to the notion of love."

With her head turned she missed the lethal chill that momentarily tightened the gaunt features.

"Even a woman with remarkable wits can be blinded by her passions. You would do well to avoid the companionship of Mr. Ravel," he persisted.

Being recalled of the passions that had been stirred to life only that afternoon did nothing to improve Simone's temper. She did not want to believe she could ever be at the mercy of her desire. Not even for a gentleman who possessed the unearthly beauty of an angel and the seductive charm of a devil.

"It is very kind of you to concern yourself with my welfare, but I prefer to make my own judgments about others," she said in tones that defied argument.

"But of course," he agreed in oily tones that held only

a hint of disapproval. "I merely sought to warn you of the dangers."

"That is very kind, but hardly necessary. I am quite capable of caring for myself." With a surge of relief Simone noted the elderly woman who was waving at her in an imperious manner. "If you will excuse me I must have a word with Lady Stewart."

"Simone." He reached out to grasp her arm, his lips thinning as she hastily eluded his touch. "I wish you to know that you can turn to me in time of need. You have only to send for me and I will come."

She gave a distant nod, wishing only to be free of his disquieting presence.

"I will remember. Excuse me."

Cold, naked fury raced through Tristan as he watched the chit turn to rush away.

To think he was being denied the glory that was due to him because of this stupid wench was nearly unbearable. She was a mortal. Mere fodder for the greater race of vampires. And yet, because of blasted Nefri he was forced to treat her as if she were more than a source of blood for his feeding. Galling enough in itself, but to also add insult was the knowledge she was no closer to handing over the Medallion than when he had first discovered her a month before.

And now, Gideon had arrived.

He gave a low growl that sent a mincing dandy tumbling down the stairs in sudden fright.

With a flowing movement he turned to make his way back down the stairs, ignoring the crowd that unthinkingly melted out of his path.

He would not be thwarted. Not by an insignificant mortal or a vampire who had grown weak and content behind the Veil.

It was unthinkable.

And he intended both of them to know just how grave a mistake they had made in crossing his will.

A smile that would have chilled the most hearty of souls touched his thin lips as he left the theater and turned into a nearby alley. Within moments a ragged man shambled forward. Tristan grimaced at the smell of unwashed body and gin. On the next occasion he Inscrolled a slave, he would ensure it was not such a pitiful specimen, he told himself.

"Come," he ordered as he moved toward the carriage he had left down the street. "Did you follow him?"

Staggering behind, the slave gave a low grunt. "Yes."

"You remember how to find his lodgings?"

"Yes." The slave halted as if he would turn and show the way to Gideon's lodging at that moment.

"Not now, you twit," Tristan gritted without ever slowing his pace. "It is time for pleasure."

"Ahhh. Hunting." The one-time mortal gave an eerie chuckle.

Tristan sucked in a deep breath, coldly controlling

the rage that swept through him. Tonight would not be a blind savage feasting that would satisfy his hunger. He had a purpose to his hunt.

Of course, that did not mean he could not enjoy the fruits of his labor.

"Can you smell it?" he murmured as his fangs lengthened in anticipation of the kill.

"Blood."

"How I have missed that arousing scent. And the power." He allowed himself to briefly savor the addictive force that churned through his body. "Ah yes, the power that will be all the greater once I have dealt with Lady Gilbert." A bleak, soulless sneer curved his lips. "A tasty morsel that I shall enjoy to the fullest. But for now . . . a harlot to quench my thirst."

Chapter 3

"They say he is in line for a crown," Mary Garrett breathed, her avid gaze hungrily regarding the powerful elegance of Mr. Ravel as he twirled a giddy Lady Woodson about the dance floor.

Simone gave a small sniff as she waved her satin fan until her golden curls bounced in the breeze. She had not seen the aggravating gentleman for the past two days, and the realization that she had spent each day in an agony of nervous tension awaiting his arrival, made her long to break something.

His arrogant neck preferably, she pettily acknowledged.

"Every foreign gentleman claims to be in line for a crown," she retorted, her own gaze fastened onto the male body attired in black as it moved with uncanny grace.

Less than a week ago she thought that she knew all there was to know of men.

They were as a rule easily managed. Allow them to believe that you found them fascinating, charming and desirable and they would readily be clay in her hands. Especially when they had hopes of seducing her.

But Gideon . . .

He refused to follow the pattern she had come to expect. He did not treat her as a delicate flower he longed to pluck. Nor did he readily dance to her tune. Instead he had thrust his way into her life, seared her with his touch and then waltzed away as if she were thoroughly irrelevant.

Her teeth suddenly gritted.

No one was allowed to dismiss her with such disregard, she told herself. Not again.

Unaware of her dark thoughts, Mary, a lovely widow with sable hair and curvaceous form, heaved a longing sigh.

"Perhaps, but they do not all possess the means of purchasing a home in Mayfair. And certainly none other is blessed with such indecent beauty. I would give my diamond necklace for an evening in his arms."

Her teeth gritted even tighter.

The thought of Gideon in the grasp of the insatiable widow was not at all pleasing.

A ridiculous weakness she was not about to reveal.

No one would be allowed to know the manner Mr. Ravel preyed upon her mind.

No one.

"You could always make him the offer," she said, her fan fluttering until it threatened to fly from her fingers. "I have heard the rumor that he is on the hunt of a fortune."

"An absurd rumor, unfortunately," Mary bemoaned. "He has been spreading enough money about town to reassure the most suspicious of matrons that he is deep in the pocket. I assure you if he were in the market I would have already purchased his services." There was a faint pause as Mary turned to regard her with knowing brown eyes. "If you had not snatched him up first."

Simone stiffened in shock. "Me?"

Although five years older than Simone, the widow had taken her under her wing when she had first arrived in London. She had not only helped Simone establish her image as the "Wicked Temptress," but she had helped to choose the select circle of friends that would ensure her success.

She did, however, possess an uncanny habit of speaking her mind with amazing frankness.

"I have seen how your gaze follows him."

Simone gave a loud sniff. "He is arrogant, opinionated and far too aware of his own charms."

Mary gave a low laugh as her gaze returned to the ebony-haired gentleman.

"What does that have to do with anything? He is delectable."

"He is passable, I suppose."

"You do not fool me. You are no more immune than the rest of us poor females."

Simone's eyes darkened. Unlike Mary she did not allow herself to be prey to her desires. She did not tumble into lust with each new gentleman who appeared upon the horizon, nor did she readily entangle herself in sordid affairs.

Not even with a gentleman who made her skin tingle and her heart race.

She remained in complete control of herself at all times.

Complete control.

"I assure you that I am utterly immune," she retorted in tight tones. "Although . . ."

Mary regarded her with a hint of curiosity. "What?"

"I would not deny a desire to challenge that male arrogance. He is far too confident that he is irresistible."

"Perhaps because he is irresistible," Mary pointed out.

"Fah."

The dark eyes sparkled in a taunting manner at Simone's confident manner. "Pretend to yourself if you wish, Simone, but do not be surprised to discover yourself burned after toying with such dangerous flames."

For no reason at all Simone felt a swirl of unease rush through her stomach.

She did not wish to be reminded of the danger that shimmered about Mr. Ravel like a cloak of warning. He had offered a challenge that she could not ignore. Not without appearing a coward. Something she could not bear.

"Save your sympathies for Mr. Ravel. He will be in

need of them," she said in tones far more daring than she felt.

Mary laughed in open disbelief. "We shall see."

"We shall, indeed." Simone snapped her fan shut as the music came to an end. It was time to teach Mr. Ravel she was not to be so easily discounted, she told herself, even as a tiny voice in the back of her mind warned her she was being a fool. "Excuse me."

Keeping her gaze covertly trained upon the elegant gentleman, Simone threaded her way through the guests that filled the ballroom. She determinedly ignored those who attempted to attract her attention as she angled toward the dance floor directly in the path of Mr. Ravel. He had managed to avoid her for the past hour. He would not be allowed to escape upon this occasion.

Hoping that no one could note the rapid beat of her heart or the manner her hands clutched the folds of her crimson silk gown she stepped directly in front of him.

With a graceful ease he managed to halt and offer a smooth bow before rising and regarding her with his midnight gaze.

"Ah, Lady Gilbert."

Simone forgot to breathe.

Lost in the dark beauty of his eyes Simone felt the tangible power of him reach out to wrap about her. It feathered over her skin and tugged at something deep within her. Fierce, shimmering heat flared through her, making her knees weak and her mouth dry.

Botheration.

No man should be able to affect her so deeply.

Not by just being near.

It was indecent.

Desperately attempting to remind herself of the reason she sought him out in the first place, she plastered a stiff smile to her lips.

"Mr. Ravel."

The sculpted lips curved as he slowly surveyed her slender form, lingering with obvious interest on the low cut of her neckline before returning to her flushed features.

"I trust you are enjoying your evening?"

Forcing her stiff muscles to relax, Simone opened her fan to slowly cool her heated cheeks.

She was the one in command, she reminded herself sternly.

It was time she began commanding.

"'Tis much like any other ball," she retorted with a bored glance about the glittering room. "The same guests, the same gossip, the same predictable flirtations."

A raven brow lifted in unspoken mockery. "You are bored?"

"More resigned," she drawled. "I continue to hope that I might encounter one who is willing to toss aside the conventional expectations. Unfortunately there are so few in society willing to be more than mindless sheep following the flock."

"You would prefer wolves to sheep?"

"They would most certainly add a bit of spice to the dull evening."

The pale, beautiful features hardened at her taunting words. "You do not know of what you speak. Be glad you are surrounded by harmless sheep. They at least do not threaten to devour you."

The rough velvet voice struck a chill in her heart before she was giving a determined shake of her head.

These vague innuendos were becoming wearisome. She had enough true worries to plague her mind without jumping at shadows.

"I suppose you are referring to the mysterious danger you have elected yourself to protect me from?"

He stepped closer, not at all amused by her flippant tone.

"I speak of the foolishness of toying with matters beyond your comprehension."

There was something so patronizing in his manner that Simone instinctively stiffened.

"Your arrogance continues to astonish me. I do not need to be warned as if I were a child."

"But you are a child in many ways despite your attempts at sophistication."

That was it.

Simone nearly broke her fan in half as she struggled to maintain her composure.

A child?

How dare he?

The most elusive, handsome and charming of London gentlemen battled for just a smile. She was toasted as an Incomparable.

Oh yes, he was certainly overdue for a well deserved lesson in how to treat a lady.

She lowered her lashes so that she could peer beneath them in a coy manner.

"Perhaps you should regard me a bit closer, Mr. Ravel. I can assure you that I am a fully mature woman."

A dangerous stillness pooled about him as he deliberately glanced back down to the vast amount of skin revealed by the crimson gown.

"You wish to challenge me?" he at last purred in silky tones, reaching without warning to grasp her elbow and steer her toward a distant door. "Very well."

"What?" Simone stumbled over her skirts as she found herself being easily forced through the crowd. "Where are you taking me?"

He glanced down at her with a sardonic smile. "You requested that I regard you a bit closer; I can hardly do so in the midst of a crowded ballroom."

Simone's eyes widened. Surely he did not think she was going to actually allow him to . . . to view more than was already on display?

"I believe you misunderstood me, sir," she said in breathless tones. She might be an expert in flirtatious banter, but that was as far as her skills extended.

The dark gaze seared into her wide eyes. "Are you frightened, my dear?"

"Of course not," she hastily denied.

"You prefer to remain here and graze among the sheep?"

There was no missing the challenge in his voice and Simone bit her bottom lip. It was one thing to calmly plot to bring this gentleman to heel, it was quite another to be whisked out of the ballroom and perhaps find herself treading waters that were far more dangerous than she had expected.

Only the hint of smug superiority in the dark eyes forced her to thrust aside the shivers of warning that raced through her.

"No."

Something indefinable smoldered to life in the midnight eyes at her simple word.

"Then come along."

His grasp tightened and with extraordinary ease he managed to clear a path and lead her onto the darkened terrace. He did not halt as she had expected but continued toward the stairs that led to the shadowed garden. In silence they followed the narrow trail that at last ended in a circle of marble benches with a fountain in the center.

The sultry heat surrounded them, the music only faintly audible as they slowed to a halt beside the fountain. Hoping to hide her unease, Simone pulled away and trailed her fingers through the water in the marble basin.

It was the perfect opportunity to weave her spell of seduction, but she found it oddly difficult to conjure the flirtatious manner that came so easy when in the company of most gentlemen.

Of course when she was in the company of other men the air did not feel so thick she could barely breathe and her stomach did not quiver as if frantic butterflies were battling to be released, she acknowledged wryly.

Feeling the prickles of awareness as his gaze swept over the long curtain of golden curls she had left loose to tumble about her shoulders, she reluctantly lifted her head.

She could not stand here like a nitwitted schoolgirl forever.

"I believe I should tell you that I was warned to beware you by an old acquaintance of yours," she at last murmured, unable to conjure anything remotely clever to say.

Bathed in silver moonlight the refined features appeared to harden at her words.

"Were you?"

"Yes, a Mr. Soltern."

An odd ripple seemed to stir the air as the midnight eyes abruptly narrowed.

"I see. And what did he tell you?"

Simone absently rubbed the rash of bumps upon her arms, sensing the tension that flowed from Gideon. Not for the first time she wondered precisely what had occurred between this gentleman and Mr. Soltern to create such animosity.

"That you were less than honest, with hidden motives in seeking me out. He also implied you were a fortune hunter."

His smile held a grim determination. "I am, indeed, a hunter, but not of fortune."

She eyed him warily, for the moment forgetting the reason she had allowed herself to be lured to the garden.

"Then what do you hunt?"

His gaze briefly lifted to sweep through the darkness that surrounded them, almost as if he were searching for someone, or something.

"Those who would seek to destroy my home," he at last retorted in fierce tones.

Simone frowned at the mysterious words. Did he speak of a traitor to his country? Or a personal enemy that sought to harm his family?

"This Mr. Soltern is one you hunt?"

"Yes."

She considered him for a long moment, wishing he were not so terribly clever at hiding his emotions. The pale, perfect features gave nothing away.

"What does this have to do with me?"

The dark gaze abruptly returned to her face, the uneasy tension fading as he allowed that mocking smile that so annoyed her to return to his lips.

"The time is not yet right to reveal such information."

Feeling as if she had neatly been put into her place, Simone eyed him with a jaundiced frown. She wondered if he was deliberately offensive to keep her at a distance or if it was simply his nature.

"Fah." She snapped open her fan. "You wrap yourself in mystery in the hopes of beguiling me."

The dark brows rose in a taunting fashion. "I need no mystery to beguile you, my love. There are far more pleasurable means of doing so, if I chose."

Her teeth clenched. "Is that so?"

"Shall I demonstrate?"

He stepped closer and Simone momentarily battled the urge to flee to the safety of the ballroom. Those earlier shivers of dark excitement returned as she felt the heat of him caress her bare skin.

Hoping she appeared far more assured than she felt, she gave a lift of one shoulder.

"If you wish."

"Actually I am confident it is your wish," he audaciously retorted, lifting a slender finger to trail it down the low cut of her neckline. "I would not desire to disappoint you."

Her eyes widened, as much as from the shocking heat that flared through her body at his touch as by the arrogance of his claim.

"Why, you . . ."

She had not quite decided upon the proper insult for his outlandish behavior, but in the end it did not matter as he abruptly lowered his head and claimed her lips in a branding kiss.

All thoughts faded as she was struck by a bolt of lightning that singed her from her lips to the tips of her curled toes.

Shimmering heat cloaked about her and the faint scent of . . . what was it? Cinnamon? A musky spice that clouded her thoughts and filled her senses. She leaned heavily against his hard, chiseled form as her knees became weak. His mouth moved with a practiced skill and Simone gave a low moan of pleasure.

She shivered as a potent desire flooded her body. His hands molded her ever closer, making her vibrantly aware of every hard curve and plane of his muscular form. She opened her lips, allowing him ready access to the moist warmth of her mouth.

This was what she had sensed between them from the beginning, she acknowledged dizzily.

This fierce, blazing hunger that threatened to consume them both.

She knew she should be terrified. This was not what she had planned at all. He was the one who was supposed to be lost in a haze of need.

Still, it was not until those clever fingers slid upward to lightly cup the fullness of her aching breast that she came to her fogged senses.

A pleasure that she had never before dreamed existed

exploded deep within her, making her sharply pull away in shock.

Dangerous waters, indeed.

Licking her tingling lips she regarded him with wide, startled eyes. His own expression was much more difficult to read, although there was no missing the thick tension that smoldered in the air.

"You tremble in my arms," he at last murmured in smoky tones.

"I . . ." Determined to deny his arrogant charge, the words stuck in her throat.

"Yes, my temptress?" he prodded.

The lie would not come and she sucked in an unsteady breath. Surely it was not cowardly to realize when it was best to retreat? There would be other nights to teach this gentleman a lesson he so richly deserved, she attempted to ease her damaged pride. And on the next occasion she would be prepared to battle those dizzying sensations that threatened to overwhelm her.

"We should return to the ballroom," she managed to say in a husky voice.

His lips twitched as if he were fully aware of the heat that still tormented her.

"But I have not yet fully beguiled you." His accent was more noticeably pronounced as he reached out to gently stroke his hand down the curve of her neck. The dark eyes smoldered with an unreadable fire as she shivered beneath his caress.

"We will be missed," she breathed.

"I thought you shunned society's rules?"

Those fingers brushed the frantic pulse at the base of her neck, the moonlight adding dangerous shadows to his lean countenance. He suddenly appeared different.

Harder.

Perilous.

Inflexible.

A predator that could destroy her with ease.

"Gideon?"

"Do you still prefer to be among the wolves?" he demanded, his dark velvet voice sending a shudder through her. "There is danger here in the dark."

Simone readily believed him.

She could feel the danger.

It pulsed in the still air and cloaked about her slender body. She suddenly felt vulnerable in a manner she had never before experienced.

"This is madness," she whispered more to herself than to the gentleman watching her with those glittering eyes.

"Then remain with the sheep where you are safe, my dear."

The challenge was unmistakable, but for once Simone was not so swift to rise up and meet it.

She had her pride, but she was not a complete fool.

"I . . ."

The sudden sound of approaching footsteps was almost

a welcome intrusion and ignoring the taunting smile that curved his mouth, Simone readily turned to watch the uniformed servant who hurried in their direction.

"Pardon me for intruding, Mr. Ravel," the young footman apologized with a low bow.

Gideon waved a pale hand. "What is it?"

"A message arrived for you. The servant claimed that it was urgent you speak with him."

"Thank you." Waiting for the footman to turn and make his way back toward the house, Gideon shifted so that he could stab her with a piercing gaze. "It seems our interlude must come to an untimely end. You can find your way back to the ballroom on your own, I trust?"

Simone lifted her brows in surprise, forgetting that just a moment before she was anxious to end her time alone with Gideon. She was not accustomed to being dismissed with such obvious ease.

"You are leaving?"

He gave a shrug. "Duty calls."

"Duty? What duty?" she demanded, regarding him with suspicion. "Where are you going?"

He reached out to tap her nose as if she were a precocious child rather than the "Wicked Temptress" who had bewitched London with her seductive powers.

"Out among the wolves, my love," he murmured, leaning down to tenderly brush her lips before he was disappearing into the shadows with a fluid motion.

Feeling baffled and more than a bit dazed by her latest

encounter with Mr. Ravel, Simone planted her hands upon her hips and glared into the darkness.

Nothing had gone as it was supposed to.

Gideon was no closer to being wrapped in her silken threads of power while she . . . well, there was no denying that she had eagerly fallen into his arms like an overripe peach.

What had Mary said earlier? Something about being burned when playing with fire?

Her eyes narrowed with self-recrimination. She had failed on this occasion. Failed spectacularly.

Next time, she silently assured herself.

And there would be a next time.

Chapter 4

Gideon glided through the shadows with a frown marring his wide brow.

He was not at all happy to discover that it had been more than a little difficult to leave Simone behind in the garden.

It had, indeed, been a decided wrench.

For the love of great Nefri, she was a mortal, he reminded himself sternly.

A mere woman who was only important because she briefly held a part of the Medallion.

But when he had pulled her into his arms and touched his lips to hers, he had forgotten the reason he was determined to keep her close. He had forgotten that he intended to use her passions to weave a trap she could not escape. He had forgotten all but the sweet temptation that had flooded through him.

His frown deepened as he angled toward his waiting carriage.

He was well acquainted with passions of the flesh.

He had lost himself in the pleasures of mortal women on countless occasions before retreating behind the Veil.

But this was nothing at all like he remembered.

Oh, there was the same burning hunger that raced through his blood, and the same ache that hardened his body with need. But threaded through the desire was a strange, unexpected tenderness that made him long to sweep her off her feet and hide her far away from the danger that threatened.

Tenderness.

He gave a shake of his head.

There was no place for such weakness among vampires.

Only humans found pleasure in such frailty.

Ignoring the urge to turn about and ensure that Simone made it safely back to the ballroom, Gideon continued on to his carriage. Within moments the groomsman stepped forward to open the door so that he could climb within and discover the slender, ragged youth that was nearly hidden in a distant corner.

He thrust aside his bothersome thoughts to concentrate upon the lad he had hired to keep his ears open for rumors of a Mr. Soltern. Older than most of the other ragamuffins he had put into his service, the boy possessed a calm intelligence that had impressed Gideon from their first meeting.

"I presume this has something to do with Mr. Soltern?" he demanded as he slid into a seat across from his unexpected guest.

"No, sir," the lad surprised him by admitting in a near whisper. "But you did ask to be informed of any . . . unusual deaths in the city."

Gideon felt a stir of premonition ripple through the closed confines of the carriage. His muscles tightened with sudden anticipation although no human eye could have detected his tension as he leaned negligently against the leather cushions.

"There has been a murder?"

"Aye, a harlot from the Rookery."

Gideon gave a lift of his brow. "Hardly an unusual occurrence."

"The girl was found floating in the river with her throat ripped out."

With a smooth movement Gideon lifted the hatch set in the roof of the carriage.

"To St. Giles," he commanded in cold tones.

"Yes, sir," the coachman retorted with a crack of his whip.

With a lurch the carriage was in motion, traveling through the pleasant peace of Mayfair toward Great Russell Street where thieves and whores plied their trade.

Gideon returned his attention to the boy across from him. "Tell me what you know."

"T'ain't much." He rubbed the tip of his pointed nose. "I was lingering outside Mrs. Finch's establishment, seeing as how most of the fancy gents enjoy spending a few hours with her girls, hoping to catch a hint of this

Mr. Soltern when I overheard two blokes talking of a whore they had pulled out of the river. It seems the Watch was right upset when they discovered her throat was missing."

Gideon drummed impatient fingers upon his knee. Tristan had always been brutal, and with the powers of his bloodlust he could easily shift to an animal capable of such destruction. Certainly he would not put it past the renegade to enjoy such a kill.

"What do the authorities believe occurred?"

"The runners are saying it is a madman."

"Certainly a madman," Gideon agreed with a chilled smile.

The usually unshakable youth shifted nervously against the smooth leather of his seat.

"Were you wanting to see the body?"

He considered a long moment before giving a shake of his head. At the moment it was more important that he discover who had witnessed this murder. There had to be someone who had taken note of the whore. And who had been her last customer.

"There is no need. I wish to be taken to where she was last seen."

"It is bound to be dangerous," the boy warned. "Gentleman such as yerself will be seen as an easy mark in such a neighborhood."

The dark eyes glittered with a lethal glow. "There

will be none foolish enough to trouble me," he retorted in silky tones.

Something in the harsh set of his features seemed to assure the boy that he was more than a match for even the most hardened criminal.

"Aye, sir."

A heavy silence descended as they rumbled down the cobbled streets, leaving behind the tidy squares and gardens to enter the narrow, dark lanes that were crowded with gin shops, slaughterhouses and common lodging hovels. It was a maze of alleys, cul-de-sacs and closed courts that made it near impossible to travel without becoming hopelessly lost. And in the shadows lurked the desperate prostitutes, pickpockets and drunkards that clung to a meager existence.

Gideon's nose twitched as the pervasive smell of raw sewage, rotting fish and sour sweat filled the air. It was the stench of poverty and despair that was in sharp contrast to the luxury they had just left behind.

It was also the stench of danger, he reminded himself.

Having given in to his savage desires, Tristan may not be able to walk the streets during the brightness of daylight, but during the night his powers would be formidable. Far too formidable.

With a covert motion Gideon reached beneath his coat to touch the cold steel of the dagger he had hidden in a secret pocket.

"That be the street she worked," the urchin abruptly announced, pointing out the window toward a narrow alley that looked precisely the same as every other dingy and dirty alley in the district.

Gideon gave a rap on the carriage roof and awaited the coachman to slow to a halt. The door was pulled open by a footman, but on the point of climbing out Gideon paused to give the boy across from him a stern glance.

"You are to remain here."

"But, sir . . ."

"Have no fear, I shall return momentarily," he retorted in firm tones.

Confident that he would be obeyed, he slipped out of the carriage and made his way toward the alley. Ignoring the sudden hush that settled through the neighborhood he readily stepped between the overhanging buildings, his form flowing with the skilled grace of a hunter and his vision as sharply clear during the night as during the day. Such eerily fluid movements should have warned all that he was not a foolish dandy out on a lark, but as he had expected he had only to take a few steps before there was a sudden scrap on the cobblestones behind him.

"Right then, turn about nice and slow," a harsh voice ordered.

Gideon readily complied, his narrowed gaze taking in the thin countenance and mismatched clothing. Although a small, wiry man, there was no mistaking the hard edge to his features nor the gleam of a large knife he held in his hand.

In no mood to tangle with the experienced thief, Gideon softly spoke the words of power that would briefly compel the man to his will.

"I need information and you will provide it, is that understood?" he demanded in tones too low to carry.

There was a brief silence as the thief struggled to battle the spell that clouded his mind before he was giving a grudging nod of his head.

"Yes."

Gideon stepped closer, his senses fully aware to every sound and scent that filled the alley. He would not be caught unaware by Tristan. Nor any of his slaves.

"There was a prostitute pulled from the river this evening. Did you know her?"

"Called herself Clorinda, she did, but more than likely it were a name she made up to make herself sound more an actress than a tart."

Gideon waved a dismissive hand. He possessed no interest in the woman's name, only the reason she had been so flagrantly disposed of.

"Did you see her leave yesterday evening?"

There was a reluctant nod. "Yes."

"Did she leave with a gentleman?"

"She left with any number of gentlemen."

Gideon reined in his impatience. "Tell me of the last gentleman who hired her services."

Even though in Gideon's power the thief gave a visible shudder. "A fancy bloke with a cape."

"Did he have a carriage?"

"Yes, black with no crest on it. They took off toward the docks."

It was too much to hope that Tristan would have been foolish enough to leave a clue to his current lair. He would have to know that Gideon would far prefer to face him when his powers were at their weakest.

"Did you hear him say anything?" he demanded with an edge of annoyance.

"He told her to take down her hair."

Caught off guard Gideon felt those prickles of warning once again flare through him.

"Why?"

"Said he was wanting a woman with long blond hair. Seemed very particular about that."

Gideon clenched his teeth as a wave of fury threatened to destroy his cool logic.

He suddenly understood the reason for the savage, highly visible attack.

Tristan was taunting him.

The renegade desired him to realize that Simone would suffer a similar fate if he failed.

His hands clenched as the image of her slender body battered and ravaged seared through his mind. Tristan would be merciless given the opportunity to punish the maiden for standing in his way.

Far more merciless than he had been to the golden-haired harlot.

For the first time in his eternal existence Gideon experienced a sharp flare of fear.

Simone screamed as the whip cut into the soft skin of her back. She wanted to be strong. To pretend that she was impervious to the punishment her sister so readily offered. But the leather thong continued to fall, tearing open her tender flesh and sending blood flooding down to the stone floor. She struggled against the ropes that bound her hands, unable to halt herself from pleading for mercy. From behind she heard her sister laughing. . . .

Without warning Simone discovered she was no longer in the darkened wine cellar but riding in an elegant carriage. She was attired in a dark wool gown that scratched at her skin and effectively disguised her slender curves. They were traveling through the peaceful countryside but Simone felt a tingle of alarm flare through her. She knew that somewhere in the distance was a band of highwaymen that were awaiting their approach. Desperate thugs who would kill without warning. She tried to open her mouth and warn the coachman, but she could not speak. . . .

Blackness surrounded her. A thick, smothering darkness that stole her breath and made it impossible to move. Suddenly a faint, silvery image of a man could be detected in the distance. He seemed somehow familiar as he lifted a hand to beckon her closer. A cold chill struck her heart at the sight of the stranger, but she could not prevent herself from struggling to move toward him. A seductive voice whispered in her ear, promising delights beyond imagining if she would only surrender to him. If only she would offer the amulet that glowed in the darkness.

Her hand lifted toward the amulet, clutching the warm gold in tight fingers. But even as she considered lifting the necklace from her neck the image of the old gypsy woman was standing before her, the wrinkled countenance harsh with warning.

"No, child. You must protect the Medallion," she said in tones that defied argument. "All depend upon you. You must be strong. Do not be deceived by those who would destroy you. Do not be deceived. . . ."

With a cry Simone abruptly sat up in bed, her fingers tender from where the amulet had cut into her skin.

A dream.

She shuddered with relief as she sank back upon her pillows.

It was not the first occasion she had been plagued by nightmares. Heaven above knew that her past was enough to give anyone lurid dreams.

But never before had she dreamed of the shadowy form that had seemed so real. She could still feel those odd prickles that had raced over her when those seductive words had been whispered in her ear, and the desire to do whatever was commanded of her. If not for the appearance of the old gypsy who knew . . .

With a shake of her head at her foolishness Simone forced herself from her bed and rang for a bath.

It had been a dream, nothing more.

She was not yet so ridiculous that she would be frightened by figments of her imagination. No matter how vivid they had been.

With that brave thought firmly in mind, Simone prepared for the day, but once she had left her chambers she discovered herself lingering over the smallest tasks. It was not that she had been rattled by those disturbing dreams, she swiftly reassured herself. It was just that she was weary from her restless night and not at all in the mood to gad about town.

Devoting the day to overseeing a complete cleaning of the house, as well as a detailed inventory of the linens and silver, Simone ate her dinner alone and then retired to the large library to enjoy a travel book that she had longed to read since she had discovered it on a high shelf several weeks before. When she had been younger she had fantasized about escaping England and her sister to travel the world. Although she no longer felt the burning need to flee, she had never lost the faint desire to simply pack her bags and discover all the wondrous places that beckoned.

Night fell as she continued to read of the daring adventures of a young priest traveling through the Americas when she was interrupted by a wide-eyed maid who dipped a hasty curtsy.

"Pardon me, my lady, but Mr. Soltern has called."

Mr. Soltern?

Simone surged to her feet, unthinkingly allowing the book to tumble to the rose-patterned carpet. The mere thought of the cold, distasteful gentleman in her home was enough to send a rash of unease over her skin.

"Please, tell him . . ."

"Good evening, Lady Gilbert," Mr. Soltern drawled as he stepped into the library with an icy smile.

Simone snapped her lips closed as she encountered the cold, lifeless gaze. She would have her butler's head upon a platter, she thought as she battled the heavy sense of dread that suddenly filled the room. It was bad enough that Gideon was allowed to walk in whenever he felt the urge. She would not have every buffoon who called himself a gentleman traipsing through her home.

Especially not a gentleman who made her skin crawl with dislike.

"Mr. Soltern. I did not expect you this evening," she said stiffly.

He glanced toward the silent maid who abruptly turned and hurried from the room, leaving the two of them alone. Only then did he return that flat gaze to regard her in a measuring fashion.

"Forgive me for intruding, but I did wish to see you as soon as possible."

Simone swallowed heavily, battling the urge to flee behind the frightened maid. She would not be intimidated in her own home, she sternly chided herself. Not even by this man.

"Is there a problem?"

"Not at all." Without warning he glided forward and placed a small velvet box in her unwilling hands. "I have procured a small gift I hoped would please you."

Instinctively she took a step back from the frigid air that seemed to shroud about him, regarding the box with suspicion.

"That is very kind, but not at all necessary."

"I fear it is necessary, my dear," he retorted with that smile that could have sliced through a diamond. "For some reason you have taken me in dislike and I should very much wish to alter your harsh opinion."

All too aware of how alone she was with this man, Simone forced herself to give a shake of her head.

"That is absurd."

"Then I have mistaken your cold disregard?" he demanded.

"We are barely acquainted."

"An oversight I intend to correct," he threatened. "Will you not at least open my gift?"

"Very well," she grudgingly conceded, her fingers fumbling to pull the lid off the box. Her eyes widened in shock at the ornate gold bracelet that lay upon a pillow of satin. "Oh."

"It is a bracelet that was owned by Anne Boleyn."

She lifted her gaze in disbelief. "I cannot accept this. It must be priceless."

He waved his hand in a dismissive motion, carefully studying her startled expression.

"I wish you to have it. Collecting unusual jewelry is rather a hobby of mine."

"Is it?" she retorted, setting the bracelet aside with a sense of repugnance. Priceless or not, it carried with it a feeling of ill luck. A woman beguiled by wealth and power that led to her death.

A shiver raced down her spine.

She had not been beguiled by wealth or power.

Merely freedom.

"Yes," Mr. Soltern replied, his gaze shifting to the amulet that suddenly felt heavy about her neck. "And I must admit that I have been quite taken with that amulet you wear. Did you purchase it in London?"

A frown tugged at her brows. What was it about her amulet that created such interest? First Gideon, then the strange figure in her dream, and now this man.

"No, it was given to me," she said warily.

"Ah, may I inquire by whom?"

The amulet grew warm against her skin, almost as if in a warning.

"A . . . friend."

The cold gaze narrowed. "Perhaps you would direct me to this friend? I would be very interested in viewing any other jewelry the person might possess."

For reasons she could not put her finger upon Simone discovered herself unwilling to admit that she had been given the amulet by a mad old gypsy. In truth, she did not even wish to have the man staring at it in such an intense fashion. There was something decidedly hungry in that glittering gaze.

"It was a passing acquaintance. I do not know how she could be located," she retorted in all truth.

"A pity." His gaze lifted to stab deep into her eyes. "In that event, I would be willing to make an offer for that particular piece."

Her hand instinctively lifted to cover the amulet. "You wish to buy my necklace?"

"As I said, it is most unusual. It would greatly enhance my collection."

"No, I thank you. I am fond of the amulet."

The gaunt countenance hardened at her refusal. "But you have not yet heard my offer. I am prepared to be quite generous."

Simone shifted uneasily as the air seemed to shimmer with a sudden danger. She was no coward, but there was something about this gentleman that warned her that he could be ruthless when angered.

"I do not doubt your generosity. I simply have no desire to sell the necklace."

For a tense moment she wondered if he might actually take the necklace by force, then with an obvious effort, Mr. Soltern managed to replace that unnerving smile.

"Understandable. You should, however, have it studied by an expert to determine if it is of historic value. It might very well be a Roman or even Egyptian artifact. I can have it delivered to the appropriate scholars."

Simone's grasp upon the necklace tightened. He wanted the amulet. Wanted it with a craving that was nearly tangible.

Was it perhaps an artifact that was worth a fortune? Or perhaps of historic value? Or was it something darker?

"I will consider your offer," she said cautiously.

He stepped closer, his hands clenched at his side. "It is careless to wait. . . ."

"Well, well, Tristan, what a delightful surprise," a dark voice suddenly drawled from the doorway. "I did not expect to discover you here."

Mr. Soltern flowed with startling speed to confront the intruder. The dangerous prickles in the air became so thick that Simone shivered.

It was a moment before she at last turned her gaze to encounter the familiar countenance of Gideon.

For once she was not at all opposed to his ill mannered intrusion into her home. It occurred to her that he was perhaps the one gentleman in all of London who would not be easily intimidated by Mr. Soltern.

"Gideon," the older gentleman greeted in metallic tones. "A pleasure, as always."

Ignoring Simone completely, Gideon moved farther into the room, his lean form appearing reassuringly large in the silky black coat and pantaloons.

"Is it?" With a lift of a midnight brow, Gideon peered down his thin nose. "I thought perhaps you were avoiding me. You have been very elusive."

"I have been rather occupied." Mr. Soltern allowed a small silence to stretch before he curled the corner of his lips in a sneering smile. "I do trust you received the gift I left for you last evening?"

Although Simone could detect no change upon Gideon's aloof countenance, she sensed him bristle at the taunting words. She was also oddly certain that she did not wish to know what this "gift" might have been.

"As predictably tedious as ever, Tristan. I would have hoped the years would teach you a measure of finesse if nothing else," he murmured in silky insult.

Mr. Soltern gave a low, nerve-rasping chuckle. "I am sorry you were disappointed. Still, you will perhaps prefer the trifling present I discovered for you earlier this evening. I assure you that I delighted in procuring it for you."

The dark eyes flared with loathing before Gideon managed to regain control of his brief display of emotion. "A waste of your time."

Mr. Soltern's expression was smug, as if delighted at having managed to stir the younger gentleman's wrath.

"I think not. Besides, it was more a pleasure than duty."

Gideon briefly glanced toward the warily suspicious Simone before returning his attention to the gentleman standing in the center of the room.

"This is not the place for our private conversation. Perhaps you will join me at my home?"

"A tempting offer, of course, but I fear I have an appointment." Without warning Mr. Soltern turned toward Simone and swept a bow. "My dear Lady Gilbert, I do hope you will consider my offer."

Unnerved to be once again pinned by that relentless gaze, Simone gave a vague shrug.

"I will think upon it."

"Very well. I shall call later in the week." Mr. Soltern offered a slight nod toward Gideon. "We shall no doubt meet again. Now I must be off."

Moving with a supple grace the gentleman was across the room and disappearing from the room before Gideon could protest. He watched his retreat with a dark frown.

Deeply relieved to be free of the company of Mr.

Soltern, Simone drew in a shaky breath. She did not like the sense she was poised on the edge of a rapier. Nor the ridiculous desire to wash herself after encountering the older gentleman.

It made her feel vulnerable in a manner she had thought to put behind her long ago.

And she certainly did not like the realization that she had been deeply grateful that Gideon had once again rudely intruded into her home without so much as an apology.

She was an independent woman who depended upon no one but herself. She was not about to become one of those weak, clinging ladies who could not manage to make do without a gentleman to lean upon.

She sucked in a deep breath as she turned her attention to the man still regarding the empty doorway.

"I suppose I owe you my gratitude for ridding me of Mr. Soltern. . . ." Her stiff words abruptly trailed away as Gideon slipped swiftly toward the door and left her standing alone in the room without so much as glancing in her direction.

Her mouth hung open in shock at his rude departure. *Of all the nerve,* she seethed in disbelief. It was not bad enough that he had thrust his way into her home, but to disappear without so much as a word went beyond all bearing.

Did he think her home was his to come and go as he pleased?

Did he possess no manners whatsoever?

Conveniently forgetting her earlier relief at his timely arrival she planted her hands upon her hips and dredged up the most condemning blasphemy she could conjure.

"Men."

Chapter 5

No human eye could have detected the shadow that moved down the streets of London with enough stealth that the dust did not so much as stir beneath his black boots.

Gideon, however, was unconcerned with human eyes. He knew quite well that Tristan could easily detect his form no matter how he clung to the shadows. And that with his shape-shifting powers he could trap him without warning.

Still he continued to follow the faint scent that Tristan had left behind when he had fled Simone's home. After nearly a fortnight in London he was no closer to finding the vampire's hidden lair and he was becoming impatient with his failure.

No, more than impatient, he reluctantly acknowledged.

After Tristan had taunted him by providing yet another gift for him, his control had nearly snapped.

He did not doubt that there would be another golden-haired woman discovered upon the streets of London. A stark warning that Tristan was all too aware of his growing weakness toward Lady Gilbert. A weakness he would use to his full advantage.

His teeth clenched as he made his way past the British Museum on Great Russell Street and turned onto the narrow, dirty street ridiculously claiming the title of Queen Street. How long would it be before Tristan became infuriated enough to forget that killing Simone would destroy the Medallion as well? His pride and ambition were far too deeply ingrained to allow him to accept defeat gracefully.

Swiftly becoming lost in the maze of squares, Gideon picked up his pace. The haunting scent of Tristan was much nearer. Perhaps with a bit of luck . . .

Gideon ground out a curse as he entered a darkened alley and was abruptly confronted by a thick mist that reached out to strike a razor-thin cut across his cheek. His fingers lifted to touch the warm blood that welled from the slice, inwardly chiding himself for his stupidity.

He had been fully on guard and yet he still had walked blindly into the ambush. A certain warning that his growing desperation to put an end to Tristan was rattling the cold logic he had always taken such pride in.

As if sensing his self-disgust, Tristan gave an eerie chuckle as he swirled in mist before Gideon.

"You have grown slow and weak, Gideon, hiding behind the Veil. Or is it from hiding behind the skirts of a woman?" he taunted.

"You begin to annoy me," Gideon retorted in icy tones. "Show yourself."

"So that you can strike that dagger you are hiding in your jacket into my heart? I think not."

Gideon forced a mocking smile to his stiff lips. "You always were a coward, Tristan, choosing to prey on those weaker than yourself and hiding in the shadows."

The mist briefly swirled, as if Gideon had managed to strike a raw nerve.

"And you have always been an arrogant prig. However did the Great Council compel you to return to this world of disgusting, inferior humans?"

Slipping his hand into the jacket to grasp the hilt of the dagger, Gideon gave a shrug. He would not be caught off guard again.

"Unlike you I comprehend my duty to the vampires. I seek our glory, not our destruction."

"Glory?" There was a rasping laugh. "Cowering behind that ridiculous Veil like we are pathetic weaklings rather than the masters of all? These mortals should be our servants; they should bow before us and feed our lust. They should tremble in fear at the mere thought of our presence."

It was a call that had been made by more than one vampire since they had left the world behind. There had always been those who desired to conquer and enslave the weak. Tristan, however, had taken the need for conquest to near madness.

To even think he would seek to destroy the Veil and to challenge the great Nefri herself was unforgivable.

"We do not cower, we seek the higher truth that makes us superior," he said in proud tones.

The mist shimmered, cloaking Gideon in a sensation of malignant disdain.

"Fah. You are no more than willing chattel to the Great Council. You have become as meek and obedient as well-pampered dogs. And like all leashed dogs you no longer realize you are mere captives. You have forgotten the thrill of the hunt."

Gideon smoothly stepped back as his features hardened. "You believe it better to wallow in bloodlust like a savage? You are no better than humans."

"I am free," Tristan grated in angry tones. "I am out of that prison and I will soon rule this world."

His hand instinctively tightened upon the dagger. As repulsive as the thought of harming another vampire might be, he would never allow the Veil to be destroyed.

Or Simone be hurt, a renegade voice whispered in the back of his mind.

"You will return to the Veil, or you will die," he stated without emotion.

"You think you can challenge me?" There was a low growl before the mist flicked out to slice the other side of his face. "You have become soft . . . a mere puppet for the Great Council to toy with as they please. I can destroy you whenever I choose."

Gideon ignored the stinging pain that lanced through his cheek. He could not afford to be distracted. Poised for another attack, he held the dagger before him.

"Another will take my place," he said grimly. "Do you think to battle every vampire?"

As if satisfied he had made his point, the mist settled back in the shadows.

"A simple matter once I possess the Medallion."

"Nefri has ensured you will never gain command of the Medallion."

The antagonism that lay heavy in the air abruptly lightened with a near smug amusement.

"You believe I cannot lure that golden-haired harlot to my will? It is only a matter of time before she gives me the amulet. And then . . ." Tristan paused as if to savor his words. "Ah, then I will teach her a lesson in daring to defy me."

Gideon struggled to disguise the fierce fury that flared through him. He would not give Tristan the satisfaction of knowing just how vulnerable he was becoming.

It might very well be a fatal mistake.

"Your spells and powers cannot work upon Lady Gilbert as long as she is protected by Nefri."

"I have no need of spells to seduce a mere mortal," the vampire sneered, his voice echoing through the darkened alley. "Very soon she will be anxious to offer me whatever I desire. And if you ask very, very nicely I might even allow you to watch as I feast upon her."

Gideon took a step forward before he could halt the revealing movement. It was all too easy to imagine the slender woman broken and bloodied by the vengeful renegade. Without the Medallion she would be helpless against a vampire.

"You will die," he growled in rough tones.

A taunting laugh came from the swirl of mist. "How very delicious. The aloof, oh so superior Gideon, lusting after a disgusting human. It really is priceless."

"I lust to bring an end to the traitors who have turned their backs on their own people," he rasped, his fury nearly overwhelming him.

"I would suggest that you take your pleasure with Lady Gilbert swiftly. When I have finished with her I fear that she will not be nearly so lovely."

Clenching the dagger Gideon stepped forward, his features taut with simmering danger.

"Face me, Tristan," he growled.

Just down the alley a piercing scream split the night air, making Gideon stiffen with warning. Surprisingly he heard a low chuckle come from the mist before it was drifting toward the street.

"Enjoy my present, Gideon."

For a moment Gideon hesitated, seething with the need to follow the traitor and finish their business one way or another. Only the knowledge that Tristan might very well be leading him into yet another ambush made him check in his impatience.

He had recklessly allowed himself to be lured once this evening. He would not be goaded again. On the next occasion their confrontation would be a time and place of his choosing.

Replacing the dagger Gideon moved down the alley toward the screams that still echoed through the air. He already suspected what he would find. Tristan had deliberately led him here for a purpose other than taunting him.

The elder woman stood in a pool of light that came from the open door to the lodging house.

"What is the matter?" he demanded as he stepped beside her.

"Molly. She's . . ."

"Where?" he impatiently cut into her shuddering words.

She pointed toward the open door. "There."

With a thick reluctance Gideon stepped forward, his gaze discovering the crumpled form of a young woman. It took only a moment to realize that she had been savagely attacked. He could still smell the death and terror that lingered in the air.

His lips tightened as his gaze traveled over the long golden hair that shimmered in the flickering candlelight.

Tristan.

Abruptly he turned toward the woman silently weeping for the dead maiden.

"Find the Watch."

Cutting the last thread upon the hem, Simone held up the shimmering lilac gown that she had just completed.

"Oh, 'tis beautiful, my lady." The maid sighed as she ran her hands over the smooth satin skirt.

Simone could not deny a measure of pride.

The floating concoction of satin and lace was indeed beautiful and highly unusual with its clever flounced hem that revealed the ivory underskirt and the bodice of spidery lace. As with all of her gowns, however, it possessed a high back that cupped the back of her neck. She could not afford to allow a sudden shift in the shimmering material to reveal the scars that she hid.

"Yes, I am quite pleased with the material," she murmured in satisfaction. "No doubt it has been smuggled into London, but it is far too lovely to go to waste."

"Will you trim it with the satin roses you purchased last week?" the maid demanded.

Simone briefly considered the delicate gown, then gave a firm shake of her head.

"No, they are too heavy for such a gown. I believe the seed pearls will be the best."

"A wise choice, my dear," a darkly familiar voice complimented from the open French doors.

Spinning about, Simone confronted the intruder with an exasperated frown. Attired yet again in black with a smoke-gray waistcoat and snowy white cravat and with his ebony hair tied at the nape of his neck he appeared annoyingly refreshed—while she knew that she was pale and her eyes shadowed from a sleepless night.

The disturbance of having Mr. Soltern in her home, combined with Gideon's abrupt departure had been unnerving enough without risking a return of the nightmares that had begun to plague her. She had spent most of the long night pacing the floor of her chamber, or peering out of her window with a disturbing sense that she was being watched by unseen eyes.

She had hoped that a morning spent finishing the lovely ball gown would ease the tension that gripped her. There was something very relaxing in simply working with her hands. Now, she felt that foreboding returning.

Gideon was trouble walking.

Whenever he appeared her nerves were certain to be shredded and left raw. Not to mention the vague sense of danger he carried with him.

And yet . . .

Yet, she could not deny a swirl of sheer excitement that raced through her as she met that midnight gaze. She suddenly felt more alive, more vibrantly aware of being a woman in his presence.

He might be trouble, but she could not deny a burning desire to brand him as her own. She wanted to ensnare him to her will, and ensure he was incapable of walking away.

It was all vastly confusing.

"Gideon," she forced herself to greet him as he calmly stepped into the room and regarded the piles of discarded material and scraps of lace. "It is customary to arrive at the front door and await to have yourself announced. Do you possess no sense of gentlemanly behavior at all?"

He shrugged as he lifted his head to offer her a faint smile. "Very few."

Knowing it was impossible to shame him into leaving, Simone waved a hand toward the curious maid. She did not wish her servants to realize she was nearly always at the mercy of this arrogant gentleman.

"That will be all, Daisy."

With a longing glance toward the fiercely handsome gentleman the maid gave a swift curtsy.

"Yes, my lady."

Waiting until they were alone, Simone folded her arms around her waist.

"Well, now that you are here, what do you want?"

Rather than answering her question Gideon reached out pale fingers to lightly stroke the satin of her ball gown.

"Quite striking. You will be breathtaking in this, of course. The obvious question is why."

She frowned at his low words. "What?"

The dark gaze abruptly rose. "Clearly you have a fortune to lavish upon yourself. Why would you choose to sew your gowns as if you were a pauper?"

Simone determinedly kept her features expressionless. She had managed to keep her lack of a modiste a secret since coming to London. She could not allow all her efforts to be ruined now.

"It is a task I enjoy."

He dismissed her words with an elegant wave of his hand. "I do not doubt you enjoy the task, you are very talented, but that does not explain why you would willingly perform such a menial chore. Ladies such as yourself are very careful to maintain the image of utter leisure."

Her jaw set at his unwelcome probing. Unlike most decent people she encountered he would not be bound by common manners. She was uncertain that he possessed any manners, common or otherwise.

"What I do with my own time is no one's concern but my own, surely?"

"What is it you hide, Simone?" he demanded softly.

"Hide? I have nothing to hide." She regarded him with a challenging gaze. "You are the one who wraps yourself in mystery."

He regarded her for a long moment before his gaze deliberately narrowed.

"I will have the truth from you eventually."

Simone refused to acknowledge the faint shiver of

warning that feathered over her skin. Nothing short of death would ever make her confess her past. Nothing.

"Why are you here?" she said in clipped tones.

As if sensing she had firmly dug in her heels, Gideon favored her with a lift of his brows, but thankfully followed her lead.

"I wished to make amends."

Simone couldn't prevent her startled blink. He wished to apologize? She would have thought the sun would tumble from the sky first.

"For what precisely?" she demanded. "Intruding into my home without warning? Attempting to terrify me with vague threats of danger only you can protect me from? Or arrogantly presuming I desire you?"

Not surprisingly her taunts made not the slightest impression in his cool composure. She was uncertain what it would possibly take to actually ruffle this man.

Absently toying with the heavy gold ring he wore upon a slender finger, he strolled toward her.

"I do not consider my occasional visits as intrusions and I assure you that the danger that surrounds you is very real. And as for my arrogance"—he gave a lift of one broad shoulder—"there is nothing arrogant in the truth."

She rolled her eyes heavenward. "You are impossible."

"Ah, but I have not yet finished. I do regret leaving you so abruptly at the ball and again last evening. It was most inconsiderate of me."

Simone opened her mouth to readily agree he had

been inconsiderate. She was unaccustomed to gentlemen who willingly abandoned her with such disregard. Then, the realization that she would be revealing the fact that she had been injured by his careless manner halted the impulsive words. Instead she forced a bland smile to her lips.

"Did you leave abruptly? How odd. To be honest, I hardly noticed."

"You did not notice?" An unmistakable hint of amusement smoldered in the dark eyes.

"No." She paused before curiosity overcame her pride. "Although I am intrigued of this duty you spoke of. I suppose it is dreadfully important?"

"A tedious business that would not interest you. Besides, at the moment, my only duty is devoting a few hours to a beautiful woman," he retorted with smooth charm.

Her lips thinned. She wondered if she would ever learn anything of the man beneath his cool sophistication.

Or why it was so important that she should.

"That is no answer."

He glanced toward the forgotten ball gown upon the table. "It is as good an answer as why you choose to make your own gowns."

The thrust slid home with annoying ease.

He did not have to say he was not about to reveal any more of himself than she was prepared to do.

She gave an annoyed shake of her head. He was like fencing with a master.

"You have offered your apology and I accept. Is that all?"

He mildly regarded her frown. "Actually, I had hoped you would agree to join me for a short drive."

Once again he managed to catch her off guard. "Now?"

"Unless you have other plans?"

She hesitated. The man annoyed her, mocked her, and if she were perfectly honest, rather frightened her. But the lure of spending more time in his company was undeniable.

Hadn't she promised herself to bring him to heel?

She could hardly do so if she were cowardly avoiding his company.

Sucking in a calming breath she managed an offhand shrug. "No, I have no other plans."

"Good." He moved to hold out his arm. "Shall we go?"

Silently branding herself an idiot, Simone allowed herself to be led from the back room toward the foyer. It took a moment for a maid to fetch her gloves and parasol that she chose in favor of a bonnet. Then, ignoring the urge to rush upstairs and change into something a bit more dashing than the plain jade gown, she consented to take Gideon's arm once again as he escorted her out of the house and into the startling white and gold carriage, pulled by perfectly matched gray horses.

Although it was still May the heat of the sun made it feel surprisingly warm. Arranging herself on the leather seat of the carriage, Simone quickly raised her parasol, relieved when Gideon set the grays into motion, stirring a pleasant breeze.

Her relief was short-lived, however, when she realized they were not headed in the direction of the park as she had expected, but instead toward the less populated outskirts of London.

With a frown she glanced about the thinning houses, wondering what she had managed to get herself into now.

With her face adverted she failed to note the manner his dark gaze scrutinized her tense features and the unmistakable shadows that marred the skin beneath her eyes.

"You look pale," he abruptly broke the silence. "Did you not sleep well?"

Simone shifted upon the leather seat, suddenly aware of the scent of warm spices that clung to his warm body.

"I was rather restless."

"Did Mr. Soltern's visit bother you?"

She grimaced, unable to deny that the gentleman had set her nerves on edge. Even the mention of him was enough to make a ball of ice form in the pit of her stomach.

"I must admit I do not care for the gentleman. There is something very cold and rather inhuman about him."

The dark eyes flashed with surprise at her words. Almost as if he were startled she had managed to see through the shallow charm Mr. Soltern possessed in such abundance.

"Yes," he at last murmured. "He is quite ruthless."

She tilted her head to one side, no longer concerning herself as to where they were headed. Whatever her fears in regard to this gentleman she did not believe he would ever attempt to harm her.

"He hates you. Why?" she demanded bluntly.

He abruptly turned to regard the wide street, although there was little traffic to disturb them.

"We are old enemies."

"That much I had presumed," she retorted dryly. The air between them last evening had nearly crackled with danger.

"He seeks power and I stand in his path."

She frowned at the vague words, knowing it would be impossible to demand more information than he was willing to give.

"Do you believe that he would harm you?"

The pale features hardened until he appeared like a perilous warrior of old.

"Yes," he acknowledged in clipped tones. "I have warned you that he is dangerous."

"And yet you followed him last evening?"

Surprisingly he grimaced at her chiding. Simone wondered what occurred after they had left her house. Obviously something that had managed to leave a sour taste in Gideon's mouth.

"We have unfinished business between us."

She heaved a frustrated sigh. "Which means that you do not intend to tell me what this business is."

He swiftly glanced over her tight countenance before turning his attention to the road.

"There is still too little trust between us, my dear. It seems that for now we will both harbor our secrets."

She set back against the seat with a decided flounce. "Impossible man."

Rather than taunting her for her obvious ill humor, Gideon tightened his hands on the reins, his profile carved in granite.

"Tristan is a danger to you as well, Simone."

There was no mistaking the dark warning in his voice, and Simone shivered. After last evening she could no longer deny that Mr. Soltern was indeed determined to seek her out. Even going so far as to force his way into her home. She could still feel the repulsive gaze as it had lingered with open hunger upon her necklace.

Instinctively her hand rose to clutch the gold trinket that lay warmly against her skin.

"For my amulet?" she demanded.

Gideon stilled before giving a nod of his head. "Among other things."

She shivered, feeling as if she were stumbling in the dark. She was no stranger to fear. Still, in the past she at least had known her enemies and why they hated her. Now she was simply being thrust into danger with no understanding of why or when it might strike.

Very frustrating for a woman who had sacrificed everything to live a life of peace.

"None of this makes sense," she muttered.

He shrugged. "It is best that you avoid him altogether."

She offered him a jaundiced frown. "That is rather difficult considering that London society is quite small. We are bound to be tripping over one another constantly. And like you, he possesses the belief he is welcome to thrust his way into my home whenever it pleases him."

He gave a slow nod at her accusation. "So I have noted. I shall have to take means to prevent his unexpected calls."

"You believe you can?" she demanded.

"With some help."

The arrogance was back in his voice and her frown deepened. Really, he seemed to believe himself omnipotent.

"And your own unexpected calls?" she asked in overly sweet tones.

His features abruptly softened with mild amusement. "Those will continue, of course."

"Of course."

His brows rose in a taunting manner. "How else could you attempt to seduce me?"

Chapter 6

Although the unusual heat continued to blanket London, there was a pleasant breeze to be discovered in the lovely meadow that Gideon had discovered well outside of the city. There was also a welcome peace that could not be found among the bustle and noise of London streets.

Seated upon the blanket, Gideon lazily watched Simone gingerly taste of the numerous dishes he had requested be prepared for her approval. She appeared lovely, of course. Attired in a brilliant lavender gown with her hair appearing like spun gold as it tumbled down her back, she would have halted the heart of any man. But to Gideon's close scrutiny there were signs of strain in the shadows that lay beneath her eyes and the unmistakable realization that she had lost weight.

A strain that was no less for himself, he acknowledged grimly.

It had been nearly a week since he had last caught sight of Tristan. The vampire had efficiently disappeared, even from society, and if not for the two golden-haired prostitutes that had been discovered in the Rookery he might have feared that the man had quit London altogether.

It was beyond infuriating to know that his prey silently stalked through the streets, and yet not even his large band of urchins had been able to so much as catch a glimpse of him. Night after night he haunted the poorer districts of London searching for even the faintest trail of the vampire, only to return to his home bested yet again.

What was Tristan plotting?

Had he hoped that Gideon would tire of protecting Simone and return to the Veil? Or was he concocting some evil plot to lure her into a trap?

Not knowing what was going through the mind of Tristan was far worse than any open battle could possibly be.

At least he had managed to ward Simone's house to warn him if the traitor attempted to enter, he consoled himself. He had been forced to call upon the help of the Great Council, but with their added power he had managed to lay the invisible web about the home. It had come as rather a surprise when Valkier had actually arrived to help him. The ancient, always aloof vampire more often than not secluded himself from the other vampires, preferring to study alone; but Gideon could only presume the dire need had forced him to realize that he was as much at risk as the others. He had even taken interest in Simone, asking a number of questions as to how the amulet had been bound to the woman and whether she was still in contact with Nefri. Gideon had answered the questions as best he could, unsurprised when the man had simply disappeared when he realized that Gideon did not possess the information he desired. He was not alone in claiming arrogance among the vampires.

With a shake of his head he returned his attention to the woman at his side. Although he was angered by his inability to lay his hands upon Tristan, he could not deny he had enjoyed keeping a close guard on Simone. During the past week he had devoted at least some portion of each day with her, whether it was dining at her house or taking her to the museum or simply enjoying a drive.

Of course, such constant contact carried its own share of danger, he thought with a faint sigh.

It was certainly understandable that his newly discovered passions would be aroused by such a delectable female. She was far too tempting to ignore. But the vast amount of time they were spending together only made him more aware of her swift intelligence, her undoubted courage and the inner vulnerability that she struggled so hard to hide. She was slowly but firmly entrenching herself within his life, to the point that he wondered what would occur when it was time to return to the Veil.

He gave a sharp shake of his head, not at all willing to brood upon the disturbing thought. For now the safety of the Medallion was all that mattered.

"Well?" he prompted, hoping to divert the alarms that raced through the back of his mind.

Lifting her head, Simone smiled as she daintily wiped her fingers. Over the past week she had bounced between playing the alluring temptress and aggravated maiden at the knowledge he would not be tamed. He found her confusion a delight and readily teased her fiery temper. No doubt it would have been best had she turned out to be a milk-and-toast miss who eagerly allowed herself to be led by his stronger will. But, he could not deny a decided pleasure in her vibrant spirit.

"It is unusual," she admitted as she set the now empty plate aside, "but tasty."

"It is a dish from China."

Her gaze widened in surprise. "Really? Have you traveled there?"

His lips twitched. He had indeed traveled through China, but it had been nearly four hundred years ago.

"Yes, but not for some time."

Her eyes abruptly glowed with interest. "Where else have you been?"

He shrugged. "I have traveled most of the world."

"How fortunate you are." She smiled rather sadly. "I should like to travel someday."

Gideon found himself startled by her revelation. Travel for humans was a grueling, usually tedious task. He could not imagine Simone without her comforts.

"I thought you were a creature of London."

"Not at all." She leaned back on her hands, making him fiercely aware of the thrust of her nicely curved bosom. "I lived very quietly in Devonshire for most of my life. I have never had the opportunity to see the world. And with Napoleon ravaging Europe it appears I shall have to wait."

Taming the urge to lean forward and explore the vast amount of skin revealed by her low-cut neckline, Gideon regarded her with a raised brow.

"There are other places beyond Europe."

"You mean India?"

"It is certainly an intriguing country," Gideon agreed. "There is also the Orient, Russia and the West Indies."

An unmistakable longing rippled over her countenance before she gave a grimace. "I am not certain I am so daring as to travel so far alone."

Gideon experienced a stab of regret that he could not show this woman the world. How he would enjoy watching her eyes widen with wonder at the beauty of China and the wild, untamed lands of the Americas.

"A beautiful woman need never be alone unless she chooses to be," he instead forced himself to point out. "Besides which, you do not strike me as a woman afraid to dare anything. You are very bold."

She gave a low chuckle. "Is that a compliment or an insult?"

His own lips curved at her teasing. "I suppose there

are gentlemen who would consider you to be too much a challenge. I, however, am not one of them."

A sudden glow of satisfaction warmed her eyes. "Ah, so you admit that you find me enticing."

The passions within him flared with a shimmering heat at her provocative words. Enticing? He found her captivating, seductive and utterly irresistible. Had it not been for Tristan he would already have given in to his dark urgings and made her emphatically his own.

Still, he could not ignore the dangers of allowing himself to be distracted by lust. To lose himself in the pleasures of the flesh might satisfy him, but it would also divert him from the reason he had traveled to London.

Until he had the vampire returned to the Veil, or dead, he would have to hold his desire in check.

"Perhaps I do find you reasonably enticing, but then, London is filled with delectable ladies. I am in the fortunate position of being exquisitely selective."

Predictably, a lovely flush stained her cheeks. "Is that so? Well, I . . ."

Her words abruptly trailed away, and instantly on alert, Gideon flowed to his feet. At the same moment his hand reached beneath his jacket to grasp the dagger beneath.

"What is it?" he demanded as his sensitive gaze scanned the empty field for sign of any danger.

"Nothing." Oddly she raised her hands to press them to her cheeks in embarrassment. "It is absurd."

He turned to regard her with a frown. She was certainly not a woman to jump at shadows.

"Tell me."

"I . . . you will think I am mad."

His frown deepened with concern. "I would never think such a thing. What is bothering you?"

She gnawed her bottom lip, a sure sign she was uneasy, before giving an unconscious shake of her head.

"It is just that lately I have begun to notice . . . things much more intensely."

"Things?" he prodded.

She straightened, her hands clenching in her lap. "It is difficult to explain," she muttered. "I can smell the wildflowers, but it is more than that. I can smell each flower as if it were being waved beneath my nose. And just now I sensed there was a fox in those bushes before it even scurried toward the trees."

Gideon slowly removed his hand from the dagger, his gaze narrowed with shock. Was it possible that the Medallion was somehow affecting Simone? To his knowledge a mortal had never been in contact with the artifact. Could it be that the power had brought her a small portion of the talents given only to vampires?

It would certainly explain her heightened senses and the ability to detect the spirit of life.

"Have you noticed any other odd changes?"

If anything she appeared more embarrassed as she shifted uneasily beneath his piercing gaze.

"Nothing beyond the feeling that I am being constantly watched." Her lips abruptly twisted. "Do not bother to tell me that I am losing my wits. I am well aware I must sound like a madwoman."

He carefully considered his response. Without being able to reveal the truth, he must somehow convince her that she was not merely imagining the changes within her. Nor the hope that such changes might very well protect her from danger.

"Do not be so swift to dismiss your instincts, Simone. Any soldier will assure you that he has depended upon them more than once to avoid danger," he said in low tones. "They might very well save you one day."

"Save me from what?" she swiftly pounced.

His lips twitched with approval at her ready response. She possessed more courage and spirit than he had ever before encountered in a human.

"A savage fox," he replied as he reached down to pull her to her feet. "It is time for us to return."

She shot him a sour glance at his taunting but rather than pouting she readily helped to clear the blanket and basket so that Gideon could store them in the back of the carriage. Then allowing herself to be helped onto the leather seat she calmly waited for him to join her and set the horses into motion.

It was not until they were on the narrow path that led back to London that she deigned to break the silence.

"Tell me of China."

"As I said, I was there long ago," he replied, wishing he could share his delight of the exotic country. She would no doubt be dazzled by the beauty. "I fear that it has changed a great deal since I last visited."

"It could not have been so terribly long ago," she argued. "You cannot be more than thirty."

He battled the urge to laugh. As an Immortal, age and time had no meaning to him.

"You would be surprised."

She heaved an exasperated sigh. "More mystery?"

"But of course, it is part of my charm."

"Charm?" With a sniff she turned to regard the passing scenery. "Is that what you choose to call it?"

He chuckled softly. "Sheathe your claws, my beauty. No gentleman is willing to admit his advanced years."

"Your years are not advanced, sir. Besides which, it is not only your age you will not discuss. I have no knowledge of your past, or home or family. I have yet to even encounter your cousins."

Gideon briefly considered the two vampires who had journeyed with him to London. They had agreed to meet only in dire emergency since they would all be fully occupied with guarding their particular piece of the Medallion. He wondered if they were having any better luck than he.

"They are rather occupied with their own troubles," he said in dry tones. "Still, I am certain I could arrange a meeting if you wish."

"Are they anything like you?" she demanded with a pointed glance.

"Not at all," he assured her. "Lucien is an incurable rake who is no doubt fully indulging in all the pleasures London has to offer, while Sebastian is a scholar who has always preferred a book to people."

"Do they possess your arrogance?"

He pretended to consider her question before allowing a smile to curve his lips.

"Now that you mention it, I believe that they do. It is rather a family trait."

"Now that I believe," she retorted in tart tones.

"Is all your family so stubborn and sharp tongued?" he demanded in return.

Without warning her features lost their vivid expression as her eyes dulled with remembered pain.

"I no longer have a family."

Gideon frowned at the simple words. It seemed impossible. As a vampire, all those behind the Veil were his family, some closer than others, but all willing to stand together. He could not begin to imagine being completely abandoned.

"I am sorry," he said with quiet sincerity. "It is no wonder you seem so lonely."

She gave a shrug, as if discomforted at discussing her loss. "I miss my mother and father, but the others were not worth mourning. And I am hardly alone."

"It is quite possible to be alone even when surrounded by others. You are very effective in keeping people at a firm distance."

He felt her stiffen at his perceptive accusation. "That is absurd."

"I do not think so, my dear. You harbor too many secrets to allow anyone close, so you play the perfect hostess while keeping anyone from thrusting their way into your life."

That stubborn expression he was beginning to recognize all too well settled on her countenance.

"Except for you."

"Because I refuse to be pushed away."

Her eyes narrowed. "So I had noticed."

With a smile he raised his hand to lightly tap the end of her nose. "And perhaps someday if you are very fortunate I will even allow you to seduce me."

Her eyes blazed, but thankfully she merely clenched her hands in her lap. Gideon's smile widened, inwardly quite thankful that she hadn't actually toppled him from the carriage.

It was only with a great deal of reluctance that Simone forced herself to enter the grand, but older town house located close to St. James.

It was a beautiful home that had been refurbished by Robert Adam in a Palladian style, but while Simone fully appreciated the split marble staircase with its intricate wrought-iron banister and even the paneled ceiling that graced the upper gallery, she was not at all enamored of the shrill aria that was piercing the air with painful determination.

As a rule she avoided such musicale evenings like the plague. Why would anyone with a particle of sense desire to put themself through such torture?

But the note she had received from Mary had been quite urgent, and putting aside her dislike for mangled arias and disapproving dragons she had attired herself in a rather modest gown in dark emerald and made her way to the house of Lady Falstone.

"At last." Hurrying from a shadowed corner Mary attached herself to Simone before she could reach the open doors to the salon. "I thought you would never arrive."

Simone grimaced as another shriek echoed through the corridor.

"I very nearly did not. There are few things I detest more than listening to the screeching of endless debutantes without a hairsbreath of talent between the lot of them."

Mary waved a dismissive hand toward the salon. "I did not request you meet me here for the dubious entertainments. I have something I wish you to see."

Simone blinked in surprise. "Here?"

"Well, not precisely here. It is upstairs."

"Mary, you are making no sense."

The widow tugged her away from the guests still

entering the salon. "Lady Falstone was a distant relative of my dearly departed husband and once a month I am duty bound to attend her for tea. Yesterday I arrived and she insisted that I join her in her bedchamber since she was suffering from her gout."

Simone frowned. "You wish me to see her bedchamber?"

"Actually I wish you to see a private gallery that is at the back of the house." The dark eyes twinkled with a mischievous light. "I slipped into it on my way to Lady Falstone's rooms to take a glance at the Van Dyck that has been promised to me."

Simone was not at all shocked by Mary's behavior. She made no pretense of her love for the finer things in life.

"Ah, keeping an eye on your inheritance."

Mary glanced toward the salon with a grimace. "I have never been allowed to so much as peek at the portrait, and to be honest I wished to assure myself that the hours I spend pandering to the nasty old bird is worth the sacrifice."

"Quite understandable," Simone murmured, in no position to judge the woman. "Did you find it?"

"Yes, and something else I think you will find interesting. Come along."

With a frown Simone followed the eager woman down the corridor and up another flight of stairs. She could not image anything of interest that Lady Falstone might possess, but the quicker she allowed herself to view the mysterious object the sooner she could return to her home.

She did not allow herself to consider her desire to hurry back to the empty town house. Certainly it could have nothing to do with the notion that Gideon might make one of his surprise visits.

Nothing at all, she told herself sternly.

Only a woman who had become utterly noddy would desire to spend more time with a gentleman who tied her into such knots she could no longer think straight. Or to wish for the kisses he stole without warning.

Intent on her ridiculous thoughts, she nearly ran into Mary as she came to a halt in a small alcove.

"Wait," she whispered, glancing up and down the hall. "I believe it is clear, but we must hurry."

Darting across the hall Mary motioned Simone to join her. Feeling more than a little absurd, Simone crossed at a more dignified pace, her expression wry.

"I feel like a thief. Why are we sneaking about?"

"If Lady Falstone realized I was in her private gallery she would have my head upon a platter." Mary wrinkled her nose in displeasure. "The paintings were given to her by her fiancé, who disappeared only days before they were to wed. She kept the collection as some rather pathetic shrine to his memory and not even Lord Falstone ever entered without her approval."

Simone found it impossible to believe the surly old

woman had ever cared enough for anyone to create a shrine to his memory. Especially a gentleman who had jilted her at the altar. It would be far more in character to have burned them in the nearest fire. Still, it appeared that she had once upon a time possessed a heart.

"Will the door not be locked?"

Mary gave a short laugh. "Lady Falstone is too filled with her own self-worth to presume anyone would possess the audacity to defy her orders. Would you grab a candle?"

Simone dutifully collected the candelabra on a nearby table and followed her friend into the room. She was startled to discover that it was far larger than she had expected. Nearly a hundred feet long with a modillion cornice in a coved ceiling, the walls were covered by pictures, some enormous and hung in heavy gold frames, while others were small and grouped together. There were no furnishings beyond an ornate chimneypiece and a lone chair set next to a window.

She could have spent hours admiring the masterpieces that had been hidden away, but Mary was already headed toward the far end of the room. She swiftly caught up just as Mary halted next to a small portrait that had been hung by itself in a corner.

"There."

Simone raised her brows in bewilderment. "It is a portrait."

"Look closer," Mary commanded.

Biting back an impatient sigh, Simone lifted the candelabra and studied the dark picture. It took only a moment as the soft light revealed the finely hued countenance of the gentleman for her heart to skid to a halt.

"Good heavens," she whispered. "It is Mr. Ravel."

"That is what I thought, until I noted the small plaque," Mary retorted.

Lowering her gaze Simone read the words engraved into the plaque. "Lord Ravel. Penwhick Castle. 1520 A.D."

"I assure you that it gave me quite a start when I first noticed it."

Simone's disbelieving gaze returned to the portrait, noting the heavy velvet and lace that the gentleman wore. Certainly there was no gentleman today who would choose such garments.

"It is impossible."

"It does look remarkably like him, even that gold ring he wears."

Simone gave a shake of her head, her breath oddly elusive as she searched for some hint that this was not Gideon.

"It looks precisely like him," she muttered.

"I suppose it must be a relative of Mr. Ravel's," Mary continued to chatter, unaware of the tension gripping Simone.

"Yes," she agreed, although deep within her she could not make herself accept that it was mere coincidence. She had always looked much like her sister, both of them with the same golden hair and slender frames. They both even had a similar birthmark upon their hip. But this . . . this was not mere resemblance. Every feature, from the glossy dark hair to the arrogant tilt of his chin was precisely the same.

"He looks quite dashing with that ruff and lace. Do you suppose he was as sinfully charming as the current Mr. Ravel?"

Simone shivered. "No doubt."

"Penwhick Castle. I have never heard of such an estate, have you?"

"No."

"Well, perhaps it has changed titles."

Simone was incapable of coherent thought. She had to be alone, to consider this in a rational manner. It could not be true. This could not be Gideon. At least not him in 1520.

And yet, she could not shake the disturbing tremors that raced through her body.

"I must go."

Mary turned to glance at her in surprise at her sharp tones. "You are pale. Do you not feel well?"

"I am a trifle dizzy," she replied in all honesty.

"Shall I call for a servant?"

"No." She pressed her hands to her tightly clenched stomach. "I will return home. Thank you for revealing the portrait. It is quite . . . astonishing."

Mary frowned with concern. "When you get home

have a nice, large shot of brandy. It will soon have you set to right."

Simone smiled but she feared that it would take several bottles of brandy to set her to right. She was uncertain that all of France possessed enough brandy for such a feat.

"Yes, a most tempting notion," she murmured, turning on her heel to hurry from the room.

She had to . . .

What?

Try to pretend that she had not seen the portrait? It was certainly a tempting thought.

She had more than enough to worry about lately.

But she knew that would be impossible. She had seen that portrait and nothing could alter that fact.

For her own peace of mind she had to discover the truth.

Whatever that truth might be.

Chapter 7

From the shadows of the upper gallery Gideon watched as the slender golden-haired woman slipped through the dark foyer and paused to listen for sound that her entrance had been noticed.

He had felt her presence, of course, long before she had even reached the steps of his house. With each passing day he realized that he was more and more aware of the bonds that were being woven between the two of them. Even when she was not near he could sense her in a distant corner of his mind. Almost as if she had been branded upon his soul.

His slender fingers absently toyed with the folds of his cravat.

What had brought her to his home at such a late hour?

Certainly not merely to seek his company, he wryly conceded as she hesitantly edged toward the fine mahogany staircase. She appeared far more like a thief intent on filching his silver than a woman bent upon seduction.

A pity, he acknowledged as his heightened senses caught a whiff of her sweet perfume. His passions ran hotter in the velvet darkness. They swirled through him, searing away the cool logic and leaving him raw with need.

She was here in his grasp. He had only to sweep her in his arms to have her in his chamber. Once there he did not doubt he could soon have her lingering distrust forgotten.

Then he would sate himself in her soft temptation. She would open to him with eager pleasure. And they would join in passions as ancient as time.

Shockingly Gideon realized that his fangs had lengthened even as his body stirred. He wished to believe it was nothing more than the potent bloodlust that lay within every vampire, but he could not make the explanation ring true. He did not desire to feast upon Simone's blood and watch her die in his arms. The mere thought was abhorrent to him. But if he were to merely taste of her blood and to blend it with his own, they would be eternally linked together. Two souls intertwined . . .

He gave a sharp shake of his head.

It was not entirely unheard of for a vampire to link with a human. It was rare, however. Not only because a human's life span passed within the blink of an eye, but the sheer intimacy of the links had the possibility of overwhelming a mere mortal.

Possible or not, he had no intention of sharing the Immortal Kiss with Simone.

His heart and his soul were his own.

He intended to keep it that way.

Deliberately battling the need that threatened to rage out of control, Gideon forced himself to consider the intruder with cool reason.

Something must have prompted this midnight visit. Something more than mere curiosity. She was far too aware of the heavy price she would pay if it were known she were visiting a gentleman's house at this hour to take such a risk without a pressing reason.

In patient silence he waited in the shadows as she slowly climbed the stairs. A faint frown marred her brow, as if she could sense him, but common sense was assuring her that she must be mistaken. He smiled wryly as he realized that she must find the tugs of awareness even more disturbing than he. He suspected that the Medallion had heightened her senses on more than one level.

He waited until she was fully upon the landing before he slid from the shadows as silent as a ghost.

Not surprisingly she nearly tumbled back down the staircase before she caught the railing and glared at him with open indignation.

"Gideon, you nearly frightened me to death," she accused in sharp tones.

His lips twitched with amusement at her blustering. Even in the darkness he could detect the warm color that stained her cheeks.

"Forgive me, my dear."

She nervously adjusted the folds of her black gown. "Really, it is too bad of you to sneak up on people in such a fashion."

He arched his brows at her audacity. "I hardly believe you are in the position at the moment to give me lessons in manners, do you, Simone?"

"Well." She licked her lips, obviously searching her mind for some means of explaining her bold behavior. "There is no need to skulk about in the shadows."

"I thought my home was being invaded by a thief. Would you have me offer myself to a desperate thug?"

Again she twitched her skirts, covertly glancing toward the stairs before reluctantly accepting that she could not possibly flee before she would be caught.

With a smothered sigh she turned to meet his glittering gaze.

"I thought that you were attending the Claredon ball."

He shrugged, shifting so that he was towering over her slender form. "Without you in attendance it was swiftly too tedious to endure. I considered calling upon you, but I decided it was far too advanced in the evening."

She rubbed her hands over her arms, as if able to sense the prickles of tension that filled the air.

"You are correct, it is very late. I should be returning home."

"Oh no, my love." Moving far too swiftly to allow her to evade him, Gideon grasped her shoulders in a firm grip. "You are going nowhere until I discover why you are sneaking through my home like a thief."

There was a brief, futile struggle until she stilled and regarded him with narrowed eyes.

"I do not have to explain anything to you."

He heaved a sigh. He did not recall mortal women being so contrary. Or perhaps it was simply this particular one.

"Simone, I am quite as stubborn as you. We can remain here all evening for all I care, although I do not believe you will wish to be seen by the servants. Think of the gossip."

Her brows furrowed in frustration at his calm refusal to obey her commands.

"Release me."

"No."

She sucked in a breath between her clenched teeth. "You are the most aggravating of men."

"And you are wasting time. Tell me why you are here."

"I . . ." Whatever lie she was about to utter died as she encountered the dangerous glitter in his dark eyes. He did not bother to hide the fact he was in no humor for her elusive games. "I wanted to discover more of you."

"Why?"

"Because you refused to tell me of yourself." Her hands tightened on her skirt. "And I hoped I might learn why both you and Mr. Soltern have taken such an interest in my amulet."

He ignored the feel of satin skin beneath his hands. This was no time to be distracted by the womanly heat and scent that filled the air.

"I do not believe you," he retorted in stern tones.

She blinked with an attempt at innocence. "What?"

"You have been curious about me for weeks. It would take something a great deal more pressing to prompt you into taking such a risk."

"I . . ."

"The truth, Simone."

There was a silent struggle before she allowed the wariness she had been attempting to hide to surface. Gideon stiffened as he realized that there was genuine fear shimmering deep in her eyes.

"Tonight at Lady Falstone's I discovered a portrait of you."

"A portrait?" Gideon gave a shake of his head. "Impossible. I have hardly been in London long enough to inspire the artists and I certainly have not commissioned a painting."

"It was painted in 1520 at Penwhick Castle."

Penwhick Castle.

Gideon carefully kept his expression bland. It had been nearly three hundred years since he had last viewed the estate he had owned in Scotland. Although remote, drafty and decidedly uncomfortable during the long winter, it had suited him when he wished his privacy.

Few vampires, and even fewer mortals wished to endure the stark simplicity of his home.

One guest, however, had prolonged his visit for several weeks to complete a portrait that Gideon had been unaware of until the painter had left the castle. He had, of course, considered following the man and retrieving the picture. But, at the time he had been occupied with dabbling in royal politics and had not desired to draw unwanted attention to himself.

Now he cursed himself for his lack of foresight.

It was always the smallest details that managed to create the most trouble.

"A relative, no doubt," he murmured in silky tones.

"That is what Mary assumed, but I do not accept the explanation."

She wouldn't, of course, he acknowledged wryly.

"No?"

She gave a slow shake of her head. "The man in the portrait is not similar to you, he is precisely like you. The same features, the same hair, even the same smile."

"I must see this picture," he retorted with a nonchalant shrug.

"It is you."

"Absurd," he scoffed. "I may be several years older than you, my sweet, but do I appear that old?"

Her lips thinned at his refusal to take her accusation seriously. Clearly she was not about to be easily convinced that she had been mistaken.

"Then tell me where you were born. Who are your parents?"

"Simone." He deliberately gentled his tone, his expression one of concern. "I believe you should lie down and rest. Clearly you are not thinking straight."

Far from being reassured her eyes shimmered with a dangerous light as she abruptly wrenched herself from his grasp. In the dim shadows the golden Medallion glowed with a fire that seemed to reflect her rising anger.

"You will not tell me, will you?" she accused in shrill tones.

Gideon heaved a sigh. The Great Council had taken care to warn him of the dangers he would face beyond the Veil. Not only from the renegade vampires, but from the dark passions that would once again flow through his blood. Unfortunately they had not bothered to warn him that the woman he was to guard was a prickly, stubborn, impossibly enticing wench.

His cool logic had never been so difficult to maintain.

"And what help would it be if I did?" he demanded in faintly weary tones. "You would only claim that I am lying."

His direct words momentarily caught her off guard before she was regarding him with open suspicion.

"Who are you?"

"I am here to protect you," he said with simple honesty. "I will never harm you."

She shivered, her troubled expression striking Gideon with the force of a blow.

"How can I trust you?"

He gently smiled as he stepped close enough to hear the sound of her thundering pulse.

"You do trust me," he said as he reached out to lightly touch the racing beat of her heart. "Here."

Her eyes darkened with sudden longing as she swayed forward.

"Gideon."

"Ah, my sweet Simone." Unable to resist the temptation that swirled through him, Gideon leaned forward to gently kiss her. He felt her lips tremble at his light caress, opening in a silent invitation that was nearly his undoing. Of their own will his arms wrapped about her slender frame, bringing her against the taut lines of his own body. He yearned to taste deeply of her, to allow the desires of the night and silver moon to sweep them into oblivion. But even as she arched toward his harshly aroused body, Gideon forced himself to set her away. The dangers of losing himself within her were too great. He wanted her too much, his passions were too overwhelming. Tristan was out walking the night. He could not be distracted. "You should not be here," he managed to say in rasping tones. "I will take you home."

For a moment she regarded him with bewildered eyes, as if still lost in the magical pleasure, then a rush of embarrassed heat stained her cheeks.

Once again she began twitching the skirts of her gown. "I am perfectly capable of returning home on my own."

His expression hardened to unrelenting granite. He intended to take her sternly to task for roaming the dark streets of London on her own at a more appropriate time. Not only were Tristan and his fellow vampires lose upon the streets, but there were any number of mortal ruffians that would readily harm a young woman on her own. For now, however, it was more important that he return her safely home.

"It is too dangerous for you to be alone in the night. I presume you did not bring a servant with you?"

Her chin tilted. "No."

He gave an exasperated sigh as he firmly led her down the sweeping staircase.

"Foolishness. I should lock you in the nearest dungeon for your own good."

She offered him a chilly glare. "That is not amusing."

"It was not meant to be," he assured her darkly, leading her across the foyer and out the door.

He paused just a moment to ensure that the urchins he had hired were indeed hidden in the nearby bushes before he was escorting her down the street toward her own home.

She maintained her proud silence, but Gideon made no effort to soften her temper. He had managed to battle back his demons of need for the moment; however, he was not at all willing to test his control on a second occasion this evening.

Not easy for an arrogant vampire to admit, even to himself.

Avoiding the various drunken bucks that stumbled down the walk toward their houses, he at last managed to bundle her to the back of her home so that she could slip through the servants' entrance.

She paused just a moment, as if about to speak, but noting the unrelenting lines of his countenance, she contented herself to a loud sniff before entering the house and closing the door with a deliberate bang.

Gideon could not help but smile wryly at her display of temper. She would not be satisfied for long at his refusal to reveal the truth of himself, but for now he could do nothing but hope that she did not allow her curiosity to lead her into more trouble. He preferred her anger to fear. That he could not bear.

With a shake of his head at his ridiculous behavior, Gideon turned and headed down the street. He still had the stews to scour before morning arrived. The sooner he could trace Tristan and be done with this mess, the sooner he could . . .

He clamped down on the alarming thoughts that raced through his mind. Thoughts of him and Simone entwined in bliss.

There were more than one means of trapping an unwary vampire.

* * *

Stroking the smooth ivory of his cane, Tristan watched in pleasure as his minions stalked the unwary maid. It was a pity that he had been forced to command them only to frighten the girl and not kill her. He enjoyed watching others drain the life of filthy humans nearly as much as he enjoyed the task himself.

Tonight, however, was not for pleasure.

After days of futilely attempting to discover some means of wrenching the Medallion from Lady Gilbert he had at last forced himself to acknowledge that it would take stealth rather than brute force to achieve his goal.

His near white fingers tightened on the cane in disgust.

Nefri would pay for his aggravation, he swore. To even think he must play these foolish games with beings that were as insignificant as roaches made his teeth clench.

He should already be ruling this world. Not sneaking about like a coward in the dark.

Watching the maid pass the high hedge Tristan gave a nod of his head. In a blinding flurry three roughly attired men bounded from the bushes and grasped ahold of the startled maid. There was a shrill scream that was abruptly cut off as one of the men placed a hand over her mouth.

Tristan waited until he was certain the woman was properly terrified before casually strolling forward and waving his cane in a threatening manner. As arranged, the servants released their hold upon the maid and promptly vanished into the shadows.

On her knees, the maid was shivering with fear. Ignoring his distaste, Tristan forced himself to reach down and pull her to her feet.

"Here, my dear, allow me to help you," he murmured in soothing tones.

"Oh, thank you, sir," she babbled, tears running down her round face.

"Are you harmed?"

"I don't think so." She gave a scared glance over her shoulder. "They gave me a good fright, though."

"Shameless louts. Shall I follow them and have them handed to the Watch?"

"Oh no." She reached out to grasp his arm in a tight grip. "Please, do not leave me alone."

Shuddering in horror at the filthy hands that threatened to wrinkle the fine fabric of his coat, Tristan firmly pried her fingers from him.

"If you wish."

She pressed a hand to her throat, so rattled she did not seem to find it odd that an obvious gentleman would bother to help a mere servant.

"Do you . . . do you think it was the St. Giles Butcher?"

Tristan hid a smile at the garish title that had been given to him by the newspapers. He enjoyed the knowledge that he had managed to send terror through the city. A terror that was only a taste of what was to come.

"I fear it might very well have been."

"Oh . . . oh . . ." the maid blubbered.

Tristan gave an impatient click of his tongue. He could not use her if she continued to moan in such a foolish manner.

"Calm down."

"But I might have had my throat ripped out."

Ignoring the powerful urge to do just that, Tristan managed to offer a cold smile. He wished to ensnare her with Inscrollment and be done, but he had never managed to learn the more subtle means of manipulating the human mind without destroying it completely. He did not wish anyone to know he had spoken with the maid. Not while she might be of use.

"You are quite safe now. Shall I escort you home?"

"Oh, would you?" she breathed in relief.

"It would be my pleasure."

"You are so kind."

Tristan shrugged. "Think nothing of it. Which way?"

Pointing down the street, the maid offered him a shy glance. "To Lady Gilbert's."

"You are employed by Lady Gilbert?" he demanded in mock innocence as they moved together down the darkened street.

"Yes, sir. A fine lady."

Tristan's lips twisted. Lady Gilbert would some day pay for the troubles she had given him. Pay in blood.

"A fine lady, indeed," he smoothly retorted. "I suppose, however, that like most beautiful women she is temperamental and difficult to please?"

"No, sir." The maid loyally defended her mistress. "She is always kind to the staff."

He gripped his cane with impatience. "Highly commendable. But no one is a paragon. Surely she has some faults? A few hidden sins?"

Obviously culled by the beautiful Lady Gilbert, the maid gave a reluctant shrug.

"Well, she does insist that no one be allowed to enter the house without her approval. She is quite particular about that."

"Is that all?" Tristan shot her a cold gaze. He would have the information he desired. "No odd fancies?"

"Odd fancies?"

His desire to do away with the idiotic wench was nearly overwhelming.

"Any secrets that she keeps from society," he at last bluntly demanded.

"Oh." She thought for a moment. "None unless you count the fact she makes her own gowns."

Hardly the shattering secret that Tristan had hoped to discover. He could hardly blackmail the woman just because she happened to make her own gowns.

Still, there was something about the unusual behavior that caught his attention.

"How peculiar. She does not approve of dressmakers?"

The maid ducked her head. "I really couldn't say, sir."

Certain that the maid was concealing something, Tristan lightly touched her arm.

"You can confide in me, my dear."

There was a pause before the maid nervously cleared her throat.

"I . . . I think it has something to do with the scars I seen on her back."

Tristan raised his brows in surprise. "Scars? From a burn?"

"No. It looked more like she had been whipped. Badly whipped. Terrible scars they are."

A stab of pleasure curled the edges of Tristan's lips. So, the stubborn woman had been beaten. Not surprising. Her sharp tongue alone should have seen that she was put into her grave long ago.

Still, he knew that such behavior was ridiculously frowned upon by the pathetically weak humans. She obviously would not desire it to be known she had been treated as a common trollop.

"I see. Who do you suppose would have done such a thing to a lady? Her husband?"

The maid nervously twisted her hands together, as if already regretting the fact she had revealed her mistress's secret.

"I couldn't say, sir. I fear Lord Gilbert had already cocked up his toes when she came to London."

He drummed his thin fingers on the cane. "And she never speaks of him?"

"No, sir."

Tristan narrowed his gaze as he considered the importance of his discovery. Mere scars would not be enough to induce the stubborn wench to hand over the Medallion. But it did reveal there was more to her past than she desired to share with others. Who knew what other secrets she harbored?

Or at least he might discover a relative or friend he could use to force her into giving him what was his by right.

"Where did she live before coming to London?"

"Devonshire. Near the coast, I think."

"Did she bring any of her old servants with her?"

The maid gave a firm shake of her head. "No, sir. We were all hired in London."

It was precisely what he suspected, although he was swift to mark the annoyance of having to travel to Devonshire to the list of grievances that he intended to take out of Lady Gilbert's fine, satin skin.

"Thank you, my dear, you have been quite helpful," he murmured, coming to a halt several steps away from the large town house. It had come as a nasty surprise to discover that a web had been placed about the property that would swiftly alert Gideon the moment he came close. A reminder that he would have to deal with the interfering vampire sooner rather than later. "I do have one request before I leave you to return home."

She glanced into his face with wide eyes. "What might that be, sir?"

"I would rather not have anyone realize that I rescued you this evening."

No doubt presuming that he was about to demand a kiss or even more intimate repayment for his services she heaved a faint sigh.

"If you wish."

His lips thinned at the mere thought of soiling himself with this pathetic wretch.

"I am certain you understand when I say that a particular gentleman might very well consider it worthy of a duel if he were to discover I were in the neighborhood."

It took a long moment before she at last gave a sage nod of her head.

"Right. No need to worry. I shan't say a word."

Briefly debating whether it would be wiser to trust the girl to keep her word, or risk frightening Lady Gilbert into full flight if she discovered one of her servants murdered, he reluctantly gave a nod of his head.

He might have further need of the maid.

"Good evening, then."

Turning, he made his way down the street, his thoughts already focused on the swiftest means of making his way to Devonshire.

Soon, he assured his raging bloodlust, he would have Lady Gilbert in his grasp.

And the Medallion would be his.

All his.

Chapter 8

The drive through the park had been intended to clear Simone's tangled thoughts. After all, there were few things more pleasurable than having a bevy of anxious gentlemen fiercely vying to gain her attention. It certainly was the best means possible of healing any wounded pride she might have felt after having nearly tossed herself at Gideon's feet only to be rejected.

But while there had been any number of suitors who had anxiously preened and strutted in her path, she had been unable to appreciate their attempts.

What troubled her was not that she had revealed the desire she had been determined to hide at all cost—Gideon was annoyingly aware of her weakness no matter how she might wish to deny the truth—or that he had thankfully brought an end to the kiss before true disaster could occur.

What troubled her was the fact that she was no closer to understanding the gentleman who had managed to bring chaos to her life.

Who was he?

More importantly . . . what was he?

Leaving the carriage Simone slowly made her way up the steps to her town house.

She had never been a woman who believed in nonsense such as witches, goblins or ghosts. She did not believe in mystical signs or those who claimed to read the future, or even ill omens.

Life had been too hard to dwell upon superstitions and the fear of vague evil. There were enough troubles without adding mythical dangers.

Now, her shrewd common sense battled to deny the evidence that Gideon was . . . was not entirely human.

A shiver raced through her as she allowed the horrible thought to race through her mind.

It was not possible.

It was utterly absurd.

There was no doubt a reasonable explanation to all the seeming mystery if only she could force herself to think coherently, she tried to tell herself over and over.

But she could not manage to rid herself of the awful sense that there was far more to Gideon than just another arrogant man of leisure.

Weary of wondering if she were perhaps on her way to Bedlam, Simone waited for the door to open before she entered the foyer and handed her parasol and gloves to the servant.

If a drive would not ease her troubled thoughts, then

perhaps a relaxing afternoon in the privacy of her garden would help.

Stepping toward the mirror to smooth the long curls she had pulled back with a simple ribbon, she had barely managed to raise her hands when Daisy came charging into the foyer with a flushed countenance.

"My lady," she breathed in obvious excitement.

Startled, and not a little alarmed, Simone turned to regard her servant with a worried gaze.

"Good heavens, Daisy, what is the matter?"

"You must come and see what has arrived," the girl breathed with an impatient wave of her hand.

Regaining command of her jumping nerves, Simone chided herself for her hasty flare of fear. *Botheration.* She had been certain that the house had been invaded, or perhaps worse. Now it appeared there was nothing more alarming than the usual gifts that arrived daily from her admirers.

"Yes, yes." She returned her attention to the mirror. "I will be along in a moment."

Disappointed, the maid dipped a curtsy. "Very good, my lady."

Straightening the neckline of her shimmering buttercup gown, Simone at last turned to make her way up the stairs toward the front parlor. It would be there that the housekeeper would have distributed the various flowers and tiny gifts that would have arrived that morning.

She possessed little interest in the offerings, but the

servants enjoyed preening over her success. Stepping into the elegant room she swiftly noted Daisy standing beside the settee and the housekeeper standing by the heavy chimneypiece with her hands upon her hips.

"Now, what was it you wished me to see, Daisy?" she demanded before her mouth abruptly dropped open in shock. Piled upon the far sofa and numerous chairs were long lengths of shimmering cloth. Satin, silk, cambric, wool, muslin and velvet glowed in the late afternoon sunlight, along with ribbons and delicate lace in all colors. "Oh."

Nearly hopping up and down in her excitement Daisy clapped her hands together.

"Mr. Ravel's footman arrived earlier this morning to deliver these."

Gideon?

Thoroughly bemused, Simone moved across the room with a shake of her head.

Of course, she should have guessed from the moment she caught sight of the expensive fabric, she acknowledged as she ran her hand over the swathe of satin in a rich ruby color. Who else was aware of her dressmaking skills? Or her love for such lovely material?

But why would he go to such a bother?

To attempt to distract her from the suspicions that simmered relentlessly within her?

To bribe her goodwill?

Or simply to please her?

Her fingers lightly stroked the black velvet. "They are beautiful," she murmured. "Was there a note?"

"Yes, my lady." The housekeeper moved forward to offer her the heavy vellum that had been folded in half.

Opening the note, Simone swiftly read the boldly scrawled words.

Trust me.

There was nothing else, not even a signature, but Simone smiled wryly.

Whatever the reason for Gideon's gift, there was no denying that he had pleased her. For the first time in her entire life she had received a gift that was chosen not to impress her with its expense or as merely an offering that was expected by society. Instead, Gideon had taken the time to think of what she truly would desire. The realization made the most ridiculous warmth flood through her heart.

"Daisy, will you have everything taken to the workroom?" she requested in husky tones.

"Yes, my lady."

Swiftly the maid set about scooping up the fabric and lace while the housekeeper stepped forward.

"Shall I serve tea?"

Simone gave a shake of her head. Her stomach had been twisted in knots since she had seen that picture last evening. The mere thought of food made her grimace.

"Perhaps later, thank you. I believe I shall read in the garden for an hour or so."

Predictably the housekeeper frowned. She held the firm notion that civilized people remained indoors whenever possible. Only savages preferred to be in the fresh air and surrounded by nature.

"Mind you stay out of the sun. It is uncommonly warm out today."

"Yes, I will," Simone promised as she left the room and made her way to the back stairs that would lead to the garden.

It was warm, as the housekeeper had warned, and Simone chose a marble bench set beneath a large chestnut tree. Arranging her skirts she drew in a deep breath and attempted to relax her coiled nerves.

How long had it been since she had a decent night's sleep?

Or had not devoted hours to dwelling upon Gideon and his secrets?

Or not felt as if she were being peered at from behind every bush or hedge?

Too long, she decided wryly.

She had thought to put such constant concerns behind her after reaching London. Oh, to be certain, there was always the vague dread that her past might come back to haunt her. Or that she would stumble and reveal the truth of her background. But such worries had always been simple to thrust from her thoughts while she was surrounded by the grandeur of her home, and the endless stream of nobles who desired to count themselves as her acquaintance.

Others could be easily deceived with enough money and sheer boldness, she had discovered.

Now, however, she could not so easily dismiss her concerns.

Perhaps she should leave London, she reluctantly told herself. To put Gideon and Mr. Soltern and whatever danger she might be in behind her. It would not be easy. She had built a new life here. But . . .

"How could a lady be so troubled on such a lovely day?"

The lilting, heavily accented voice came without warning, and abruptly turning her head Simone watched in utter shock as an old, shabbily dressed gypsy woman moved through the roses and promptly settled herself on the bench. She knew the seemingly ancient woman. It was the same gypsy who had appeared in Devonshire and offered her the amulet. There was no mistaking the deeply wrinkled parchment of her countenance, the long gray hair that hung in tangles about her shoulders or the bright rags that had been sewn together to make her skirt. Certainly there was no mistaking the deep black eyes that seemed to see to her very soul.

"I . . ." Simone gave a blank, disbelieving shake of her head. "Where did you come from?"

The old woman gave a lift of her hands. "From here and there."

"I cannot believe this." Too startled to be frightened by the strange appearance, Simone did not even think of calling out for help. "Did you follow me here?"

The woman shook her head as she reached out a gnarled hand to lightly touch the charm about Simone's neck.

"I was called."

"Called?"

"You are troubled." The gypsy shrugged as if it were the most natural thing in the world to be summoned by a bit of gold. "I am here to ease your fears."

Much to her surprise Simone felt a delicate warmth flow through her at the soft voice, easing the knots and soothing the frayed nerves. She even found the burning questions of how this woman had managed to arrive in her garden being dulled to mere curiosity.

"Very well," she found herself agreeing. "What is this amulet?"

The older woman took a moment to consider her words. "It is an ancient symbol of power."

"Ancient?" Simone recalled Mr. Soltern's implication that the necklace was of historical value. "You mean it is Roman?"

There was a crackle of laughter. "Rather older than that."

Older than Roman?

Simone realized that she was not certain she wished

to discover just how much older it might be. Instead she turned her thoughts to her more pressing troubles.

"Why do others want it?"

"The power," she said simply, her heavy ivory bracelets rattling as she settled her hands into her lap. "You have felt it. It is changing you. Making you . . . more."

"More what?"

"Of who you are."

Simone frowned. More riddles were not what she desired.

"You are as impossible as Mr. Ravel," she muttered.

Unexpectedly the narrow features were abruptly wreathed in a fond smile.

"Dear Gideon. You are leading him a sad chase, although I must say that I am rather enjoying his frustration. He can be insufferably arrogant when he is not being challenged."

Simone regarded the woman in confusion. "You know Gideon?"

"But of course. He is here to protect you."

Simone briefly closed her eyes, wondering if she had fallen asleep and was caught in some bizarre dream. When she opened her eyes, however, the disturbing gypsy remained, regarding her with those dark eyes.

"To protect me?" she at last muttered. "From Mr. Soltern?"

"Among others." The old woman suddenly frowned.

"Some that I know of and others who remain in the shadows."

Simone shivered, her fingers gripping the folds of her skirt. It was bad enough to realize Mr. Soltern wished to harm her; she did not want to think of shadowy forms who might also pose a danger.

"Please, just tell me what is going on."

"In good time." The woman reached out to gently pat her clenched hand. "You will have your answers, I promise. But in the meantime, you must protect the Medallion. Do not remove it for any reason."

Simone heaved an impatient sigh. "I thought you came to ease my troubles?"

"I came with the assurance that your danger will pass if you remain strong. And that great happiness will be yours if you find the courage to face the pain that haunts you."

The words were far too vague to hold any true reassurances and Simone gave a shake of her head.

"There are a lot of 'ifs' in your words."

The gypsy merely laughed at her sour tone. "The future is always difficult to read. This I can tell you, Gideon must earn your trust or you will fail."

Gideon.

It all seemed to come back to the disturbing, tantalizing, mysterious man.

A man who harbored dark secrets.

"I do not know if that is possible," she murmured.

"All things are possible, my dear," the gypsy assured her as she rose to her feet and lightly stroked her hair. "Believe."

With a last smile the woman turned and moved swiftly back through the roses until she abruptly vanished behind the high hedge.

"Wait." Simone rose to her feet, but she knew she was too late. The woman moved with far more speed than seemed possible. Far too fast to be caught now. Giving a click of her tongue, Simone glared at the hedge. Just when she thought nothing could be worse than fearing that Gideon was something other than human, and having frightening men like Mr. Soltern stalking her, now strange gypsies began appearing out of thin air. *Believe,* she had said. Believe what? That she was going utterly mad? "Heaven help me."

"Simone?"

Too late noting the odd prickle of awareness that had been washing over her skin, Simone turned to discover Gideon standing directly behind her, his expression one of stark concern.

"Gideon." She pressed a hand to her suddenly racing heart. "What is it?"

He glanced carefully around the garden, as if expecting to discover someone lurking about. She wondered if he had overheard any of her conversation with the gypsy.

"Has Mr. Soltern been here?"

She blinked in surprise at his abrupt question. "No, I have not encountered him in several days."

Gideon did not relax his tense survey, his entire body coiled for attack.

"Are you certain?"

Unnerved at the sense of simmering danger that cloaked about the elegant gentleman, Simone took an instinctive step toward him.

"Gideon, whatever is the matter?"

For a moment he refused to answer, then with an obvious effort he forced himself to ease the tension that was gripping him.

"Nothing," he murmured, allowing his gaze to at last rest upon her puzzled countenance. "You received my gift?"

Caught off guard by his sudden question, Simone could not prevent the small blush that flooded her cheeks.

"Yes."

"And it pleases you?"

Her usual sophistication deserted her as she thought of the lovely bolts of material that she could hardly wait to begin transforming into beautiful gowns.

"Very much."

He smiled gently. "Good."

"I . . . I was just about to have tea. Would you care to join me?" she asked impulsively.

As if sensing she was not nearly as comfortable in his presence as she would have him believe, Gideon regarded her with a searching gaze.

"Am I welcome?"

She grimaced at his blunt words. Common sense might warn her she was treading into dangerous waters, but the desire to be with this gentleman was proving to be far more powerful. Whatever his secrets, she could not shake the sensation that he would never hurt her.

"That is what I am attempting to decide," she confessed bluntly.

His lips twitched. "Very well."

Together they turned to head back to the house, Simone walking at his side while she kept a covert watch on the towering form. They had reached the open door when she noticed the undeniable amusement that was etched upon the handsome features.

"What do you find so amusing?" she demanded.

"You keep glancing at me as if you expect me to suddenly sprout horns and a tail."

Her lips thinned. "Will you?"

He lifted a dark brow. "I possess enough manners to keep them hidden during tea."

It was an absurd conversation. Still, Simone could not make herself laugh at her foolishness. Not yet.

"It is not pleasant to fear I am losing my wits," she muttered.

Without warning he reached out to grasp her shoulders and turned her to face his sympathetic smile.

"There is no danger of that, I assure you."

She grimaced. "I wish I could be certain."

"Trust me," he urged softly.

A shower of hot sparks flared through her at the feel of his warm hands upon her bare skin. The knowledge that she so readily responded to his merest touch only deepened the scowl marring her brow.

"Why do people keep saying that?"

Leaving the town house in the traditional manner, Gideon swiftly rounded the high hedge and made his way to the back garden.

Tea had been rather a stiff affair, with Simone clearly uneasy at having him near. More than once he had longed to pull her into his arms and confess all. Anything had to be better than the thick wall of suspicion that suddenly lay between them.

Thankfully, he had retained enough logic to hold the impetuous words.

Not only would the truth expose him long before he was prepared to move upon Tristan, but it might very well frighten her into sudden flight. No mortal would easily accept the presence of a vampire in her midst, not even one who had been sent to protect her. And if she ran, he might not reach her before Tristan managed to capture her.

The thought of the renegade vampire tightened Gideon's features as he slid through the shadows of the garden. It had been the unmistakable sense of a vampire slipping through the web that surrounded Simone's home that had brought him hurrying to the town house.

It could not be Tristan, of course.

After giving in to his bloodlust the vampire could no longer bear the light of day. But there had been two other traitors that had escaped with Tristan and while he had yet to catch sight of them, he could not be certain that either of them had not suddenly turned their attention to Simone. If they had not yet given in to the desire for human blood they would be as free as himself to walk the streets during the day.

And whether working for Tristan, or scheming behind his back to gain full control of the Medallion, they would be a danger he could not dismiss.

In a distant corner he came to a halt and waited for the thin lad to wiggle out of the bush and offer him a cheeky smile.

"'Ello, guv."

"Have you been here all day?" he demanded in abrupt tones.

The urchin who sported ears and a nose far too large for his thin countenance gave a shake of his head.

"No, sir. I followed the lady when she went shopping and then to the lending library."

"When did she return home?"

"I reakon it be about a couple of hours ago."

Gideon allowed his gaze to roam over the garden,

carefully scrutinizing the few places that could hide a careful stalker.

"What occurred after she returned?"

The lad shrugged. "She came to the garden."

"Alone?"

"For a time." The boy lifted a grimy finger to rub the end of his nose. "Then a queer old bird appeared in the garden. Gave me quite a fright, she did. One minute she wasn't there and the next she was."

Gideon frowned.

Although vampires could easily shape-shift when filled with the power of bloodlust, they would not be able to leave their lair at this hour.

Not unless it had been . . .

His hands clenched at his side as he peered sharply at the lad. "Tell me of this woman."

The boy gave his nose another rub. "Looked to be a gypsy to me. She had on one of them bright skirts and her hair hanging about her face."

"A gypsy?" he murmured, recalling Simone's explanation that she had been given the Medallion by an old gypsy woman.

"Never seen one afore, but that's what she seemed to be."

"Nefri," he breathed.

"Beg pardon, guv?"

Not surprisingly the boy sent him a baffled gaze. No mortal had ever heard the name of the greatest of all vampires. Even among vampires she was more legend than fellow companion. Always a recluse she had been one of the few to maintain the ancient arts when others had fallen into the lure of power that could easily be acquired by human blood. For centuries at a time she would disappear, hidden in secrecy as she studied the old texts and delved into the magic that had been long forgotten.

It was how she had discovered the Medallion and the power to create the Veil.

"I speak to myself," he said with an impatient wave of his hand. He did not know why Nefri would have sought Simone out, or what she had said, but he at least knew that she would never harm the mortal woman. He only wished that he could have the opportunity to speak with the vampire. Perhaps she could give him some answer as how to ease the wariness that held Simone. "You have seen nothing of the silver-haired gentleman?"

"Well . . ."

The boy appeared oddly uncertain and Gideon gave a lift of his brows.

"What is it?"

"Queer thing," he grudgingly replied. "I was leaving here last evening and I spotted one of the maids down the street speaking with a gent in a cape. Couldn't see his hair in the dark, but I would swear it was the same bloke. Gave me the shivers just looking at him."

Gideon was on instant alert. The vampire could

easily compel one of the servants to harm Simone if he desired, although it would hardly be his style. Tristan preferred to inflict his own pain.

"Which maid?"

"I think her name be Daisy."

The memory of a fresh-faced girl who was often at Simone's side rose to Gideon's mind. He would make sure he had a word with the maid, just to ascertain she had not been put beneath Tristan's power.

"Let me know if she meets with this man again."

The boy offered a mocking salute. "Righto."

Reaching beneath his jacket, Gideon pulled out a small bag filled with coins.

"Here." He dropped the money into the boy's outstretched hand. "Maintain your guard."

With a grin the boy gave a twist of his hand and the bag disappeared up his sleeve.

"Easiest blunt I ever made. Or stole, for that matter."

"And if you see the gypsy again send for me immediately."

Surprisingly the smile faded at his command, as if the boy feared he meant to harm the old woman.

"She seems harmless enough to me."

Gideon did not even bother attempting to smother his sudden chuckle at the innocent words.

The urchin had no notion he had been in the presence of the oldest, most powerful vampire ever to walk the world.

"Never allow appearances to deceive you," he warned.

"She's dangerous?"

"More dangerous than you will ever know."

With a nod of his head Gideon turned to leave the garden through the mews. There was still the faintest trace of Nefri's presence, but Gideon did not attempt to follow the trail.

If the vampire wished to speak with him, she would seek his company.

Until then he would have to do the best he could to ensure that disaster did not occur.

A pity he did not feel nearly so confident in his ability as he had before leaving the Veil.

With a last glance toward the town house, Gideon disappeared into the short alley.

Chapter 9

Gideon waited two days before he at last sought out Simone.

He hoped that the time apart would give her the opportunity to still her fears and perhaps even come to terms with her suspicion that he was far more than just another London dandy.

Surprisingly he had discovered it more than a little difficult to keep himself from seeking out her companionship.

He found himself brooding upon whether she was taking proper care of herself, if Tristan was even now intending to harm her, and, absurdly, if she was entertaining other gentlemen while he stewed alone in his chambers.

The realization he was behaving more like a foolish human than a sophisticated vampire did not soothe his ruffled emotions.

Was he a victim of his own passions? If so, he had only to step from his home to discover a woman anxious to become his lover. Even without the use of Compulsion. But he did not make the slightest effort to do so.

It was not passions that troubled him, he at last conceded.

But passion for one particular woman. And the oddest desire to have her near where he could be certain she was safe at every moment.

Weakness, he fiercely chastised himself.

A weakness that he should sear from his soul before it could destroy him.

The proud thought made him smile.

He feared that it was already far too late.

The weakness would not be dismissed no matter how he might try. It had become as much a part of him as his arms or legs.

At last accepting that he could no longer resist the unmistakable tug of Simone, Gideon attired himself in a black coat and breeches and called for his carriage.

He tried to tell himself he was being absurd, but the need to see her was nearly unbearable as he rattled closer and closer to her town house. In truth, a decided chill of unease was settled in the pit of his stomach by the time he had walked up the stairs and was greeted by the butler.

"Good day, Bartson. I am here to see Lady Gilbert," he said in abrupt tones.

That unease only deepened when the butler gave a regretful shake of his head.

"I fear, sir, that Lady Gilbert is still making her morning visits."

Gideon glanced toward the clock set upon an ebony- and ivory-inlaid table. "At this hour?"

"I am certain she will not be long. If you will step into the front parlor I will let her know you are waiting the moment she returns."

Feeling far too restless to meekly await Simone, Gideon nevertheless forced himself to give a nod of his head. What good would it be to dash about London in search of the stubborn woman? She could be anywhere, from Mayfair to Bond Street.

Far better to wait here.

"Very well."

At his grudging acceptance Bartson led him up the stairs to the front parlor. He entered the large room, but did not even glance toward the numerous chairs and sofas scattered over the carpet.

"Shall I have tea served?" the servant demanded.

"No, I thank you."

"There is brandy on the side table. Just ring if you need anything."

"Yes, I will," Gideon promised, pacing toward the large window that overlooked the street.

Behind him he heard the door being softly closed, and he at last allowed his growing anxiety to mar his countenance. He could not pinpoint the source of his concern, he only knew that he would not be at ease until Simone had entered the town house and he had reassured himself that all was well.

Minutes passed with the tick of the white marble clock that Simone had assured him had been personally designed by Robert Adam. Not that the name meant anything to him, but she seemed to take pride in the possession.

Gideon maintained his vigil by the window, watching countless carriages pass by without slowing. And all the while the sense that Simone was in danger continued to grow.

Where was she?

Why did his awareness of her feel muffled and tight, as if she were being forced farther and farther away?

On razor edge Gideon nearly jumped out of his polished boots when a small rock suddenly struck the window he was staring out of.

"What the devil?" he muttered, his gaze scanning the bushes to discover the filthy urchin huddled in the shadows. With a swift movement he had thrust the window open and leaned out to regard the boy with a narrowed gaze. "What is it?"

"Lady Gilbert, sir," the youth called back.

Those shivers of unease hardened to cold fear. The urchin would not have returned to the house without Simone unless something had occurred.

"Do not move. I will be down in a moment," he commanded. Swinging the window shut he turned and hurried from the room. With a fluid speed he was down the stairs and out of the house. The lad joined him at the front gate. "What has happened?" he demanded the moment the boy halted.

The usual hard sophistication the urchin liked to adopt was decidedly absent as he roughly rubbed the end of his nose.

"I was following her ladyship's carriage just as you commanded, sir."

"Yes?" Gideon retorted impatiently.

"Well, she was visiting some nob, but when she came out to get into her carriage she was nabbed by some toughs and thrown into a hack."

"Damn. I will kill him." Gideon clenched his fists as a fiery fury raced through him, not for a moment believing anyone but Tristan was responsible for Simone's kidnapping. "Was she harmed?"

"Roughed up a bit." A rather sickly smile curved the thin lips. "She gave 'em quite a struggle."

"Yes, I can imagine," Gideon said in dry tones. Simone would never go quietly. "Do you know where they took her?"

"Yes, sir. I followed the hack."

Gideon gripped the lad's shoulder. "Good boy. Show me." Still keeping ahold of the urchin, Gideon steered him toward his waiting carriage. "What direction?"

"St. Giles."

"Weldon," he called to the waiting coachman. "To St. Giles."

"Yes, sir."

Waving the groom to remain perched beside the coachman, Gideon opened the coach door and waited for the boy to scramble onto the leather seat. He was quick to join him and, closing the door, they were swiftly on their way.

Heavy silence descended as Gideon attempted to thrust aside the fear that made his stomach clench into painful knots. He could not afford to have his thoughts clouded by emotions, he reminded himself sternly. If Tristan had ordered his servants to take Simone to his hidden lair, then he would be at his most dangerous. Calm, cold logic would be needed to best him.

Staring out the window, the boy gave a sudden shout. "This be the street, sir."

Gideon gave a rap on the top of the carriage and without waiting for it to halt he shoved the door open.

"Stay here," he commanded as the urchin made a move to follow him.

The boy stuck out his lower lip in stubborn defiance. "You can't be going alone. That gang was a rough lot."

Knowing that the boy's pride in his ability to face any danger would never let him accept staying behind, Gideon sent him a steady gaze.

"I need you here," he commanded in stern tones.

"Once Lady Gilbert is free you are to take her away with all speed. Is that understood?"

"I . . ." Trapped by the charge laid upon him, the urchin gave a reluctant nod. "Yes, sir."

Certain he would be obeyed, Gideon moved down the narrow street, ignoring the various harlots and street vendors that called out to him. He waited until he had slipped into a dank, trash littered alley before he slipped his hand beneath his jacket to remove the dagger. Although he continued to hope that Tristan would eventually turn himself over to the Great Council, he knew that at the moment he would kill him without remorse.

And if he had harmed Simone in any way . . . well, he offered no bets that the renegade would ever have to worry over the Great Council again.

The fact that he had just chosen the life of a human, whether she held the Medallion or not, over that of a vampire barely made a ripple in his cold fury.

Simone was all that mattered.

All that mattered.

Pausing until he could pinpoint her presence within the dark, abandoned brewery at the end of the alley, Gideon slipped forward. Oddly there was no sense of Tristan, but he did not lower his guard. With as much stealth as possible he pushed at the door nearly falling from its hinges.

The interior was dark, with the thick stench of mold

and rotting straw. He eased into the shadows, pressing close to the wall as he scanned for danger.

It took only a moment for him to discover Simone tied to a post in a far corner. Her mouth was gagged and her hands wrenched behind her back and fastened with a thick rope. Even from a distance he could feel the terror that rolled from her in fierce waves.

Vowing to ensure that Tristan paid dearly for every bruise and scrape, Gideon moved silently forward.

"Simone," he whispered in the heavy silence. "Do not fear. I will soon have you free."

Strangely she gave a violent shake of her head, her terror only deepening.

Gideon grimly moved onward, not allowing himself to hesitate. Bloody hell, she surely could not believe that he was responsible for her kidnapping? Or that he would harm her in any manner?

Her head was still shaking as he circled the post and, using the dagger, began to cut through the ropes that bound her. Once he had her free he gently removed the gag and regarded her with a somber gaze.

"Listen to me carefully," he said in low tones. "My servants are just down the alley. I want you to run as fast as you are able out the door and to the carriage. Do not look back or hesitate. Now, run."

He gave her a firm shove, but with the stubborn perversity that was so much a part of her, she dug in her heels and turned to face him with a desperate gaze.

"No. Gideon, there are . . ."

"Run," he growled.

"You must come with me."

"Damn." Grabbing her arm he roughly hauled her to the door and shoved her through. Just as swiftly he closed the door in her face. "Now go," he ordered through the heavy wood.

A shuffling from behind him had Gideon suddenly whirling about to discover four shabbily attired men leaving the shadows and walking toward him. With deliberate movements he shifted away from the door, silently praying that Simone had the sense to flee to the carriage. There were more dangers than Tristan's henchmen in such a neighborhood.

Holding his dagger before him, Gideon narrowed his gaze. Even in the dim light he could see the blank emptiness in the men's eyes. The Inscrollment that held them had destroyed their minds, but that only increased their threat. They would perform whatever Tristan had commanded them to do without fear and without halting until they were dead.

"Where is your master?" he demanded as he slowly backed from their steady advance.

"You have come," one of the servants intoned.

"Halt or I will hurt you," Gideon warned, fluidly moving so that he could keep his gaze on the four as they spread out as if to surround him.

"You have come," another moaned.

Gideon was forced to take another step back, cursing the short dagger he held. Although the magic of the blade would kill a vampire, ironically it was no more than just another dagger to a human. He would be far better served with a sword.

If they attacked . . .

But oddly they didn't.

Gideon had taken two more steps backward before that realization struck.

Why were they not striking?

Surely Tristan would have commanded them to attack anyone who attempted to release the woman he had captured? Even if they could not slay a vampire.

Or was his intention something else?

Something more sinister?

Carefully watching the men shuffling toward him, Gideon coldly considered their deliberate movements. There was no rush to harm him, but they did seem to be intentionally herding him toward the back of the brewery. Step by slow step.

Deciding that what was behind him might very well be more dangerous than the scoundrels before him, Gideon gracefully whirled about, his heightened eyesight probing the dark shadows of the corner.

For long, tense moments he could detect nothing more ominous than the scurry of an occasional rat and the bones of some animal long dead. But just as he could feel the ruffians beginning to close in upon him he caught the faintest shimmer of power that had been woven in the shadows.

A mind snare, he recognized in icy shock.

It was a spell that had been forbidden by the Great Council centuries ago. Hardly surprising. It was a nasty surprise for any vampire who might wander unwittingly into one. Once caught there was no escape from the deadly sleep that would force the poor victim to simply waste away.

A shiver of revulsion raced through him.

Now it all became clear.

Why Simone had been kidnapped and then so easily allowed to escape. Why the henchmen did not attack, and instead attempted to push him toward this dark corner.

Tristan had deliberately sought a means to rid himself of Gideon, using Simone as bait. And rather than facing him in an honorable fashion he had sunk to means beyond all shame.

Feeling rough hands pushing at his back, Gideon effortlessly stepped to one side and brought up his dagger to slice at the nearest servant. He managed to cut the man's upper arm, but he did not even blink as he continued to grasp for Gideon. Another set of hands caught his arm and Gideon heaved him aside. His momentary distraction, however, left him open to attack from the other side and he barely had time to turn as a third villain threw himself directly into his midsection and knocked him to the ground.

Gideon's head hit the flagstone with a dull thud, and for a moment he was dazed. He thrust out with the dagger, managing to split open the stomach of the man who leaned over him, but his head exploded in pain once again as one of the men swung a cudgel to his right temple.

With blood pouring down his face, Gideon struggled to regain his footing. Although he was far more powerful than the humans, he was weakened by the blow to his head and hampered by the nearby snare that threatened his very existence.

Gaining his knees he reached out to efficiently hamstring the scoundrel with the cudgel, but a sharp pain in his side warned him that one of the two men still standing had drawn his own dagger. The stinging blade continued to rein blows upon him as the other man attempted to drag him closer to the snare.

Gideon growled in fury, fighting back the blackness that threatened to overcome him. He swung out with his blade, but without warning the man pulling at his arm suddenly crumpled at his side. He blinked through the blood running into his eyes, his heart freezing as he watched Simone swinging a lead pipe with frenzied strength. Moving around him she continued to swing until with a loud crack it connected with the remaining villain's head and he tumbled forward with a low grunt.

For a moment shock and pain held him silent as he

regarded the slender warrior with golden curls and deadly pipe, then with a low, rumbling laugh he collapsed onto the hard stone floor.

Shaking from head to toe, Simone sank on her knees beside Gideon.

Even in the shadows she could see the dark blood flowing through his jacket from the half dozen stab wounds. Even worse, his face was nearly unrecognizable as a large lump swelled until he could not open his right eye. There was a deep gash on his forehead that still bled and another she discovered as her hands brushed through the thick ebony hair at the back of his head.

It was a wonder he was still alive, she acknowledged with a grim pain that bore a hole straight through her heart. With such a loss of blood combined with the horrid blows to his head, a lesser man would have been ready for his grave.

"Hold on, Gideon," she pleaded softly, unaware that tears ran unchecked down her cheeks.

Preparing to rise and go in search of help, Simone nearly swooned with relief when a scuffling noise at the doorway was followed by the familiar forms of Gideon's coachman and a groom.

"Lady Gilbert?" the coachman called hesitantly.

"Over here, and please hurry," she said in impatient

tones, forcing her wobbly knees to hold her as she pressed herself upright. "Mr. Ravel has been hurt."

Sparing a speculative gaze at the four men in varying stages of unconsciousness, the coachman swiftly joined Simone, followed closely by the groom.

"Bloody hell," the coachman choked out at the sight of his master so badly wounded, only to give a sudden cough. "Pardon me, my lady."

She waved aside his discomfort. "We must get him to the carriage."

"Yes, at once."

With a motion to the groom, the older man bent to drape one of Gideon's arms over his shoulders then, waiting for his companion to do the same, they carefully hauled the barely conscious man upright.

It was a struggle to lead Gideon out of the building and down the alley, but with a great deal of grunting and an occasional muffled curse the two servants managed to half drag their master the length of the street and load him into the carriage. Trailing behind, Simone still clenched her thick pipe, silently praying, and at the same time keeping careful watch for any hidden ruffians.

She would not be caught unaware again, she told herself with a shudder at the memory of being roughly captured by the strange villains. Even now her stomach threatened to heave at the feeling of being utterly helpless as she was being tied to the post with no notion of what was to happen to her.

Worse even than those nights her sister would come and drag her from her bed . . .

Simone gave a sharp shake of her head as she climbed into the carriage behind Gideon. Now was not the time for such thoughts.

Somehow she had to ensure that Gideon did not die.

Sinking onto the floor of the carriage she regarded the man sprawled upon the carriage seat.

"We must get him to a doctor," she said to the two servants who both hovered in the doorway with matching frowns of concern.

"No," Gideon abruptly moaned. "Take me home."

Simone raised herself to her knees to glare down at him. "Do not be a fool. You are badly injured."

He reached up to grasp her wrist, the black eyes glittering between his thick lashes.

"Simone, I wish to go home."

"You need a doctor. . . ."

"Gads, must you always argue with me?" he demanded with a weak smile.

Allowing her gaze to lower to the shredded jacket, Simone noted that most of the blood had already begun to dry. Perhaps the wounds had not been as severe as she had first feared.

In any event, she could always send for a doctor once they reached Mayfair.

"Very well," she grudgingly conceded. "But if you die on me . . ."

"I will not die, that I can promise you," he retorted in darkly certain tones. "Now, can we please be on our way?"

Needing no further prompting the coachman and groom hurriedly shut the door and scrambled into their positions. With a crack of the whip they were bowling away from the dank streets of St. Giles and threading their way to the more respectable neighborhoods.

Simone grasped the edge of the seat as she continued to kneel over Gideon, barely resisting the urge to trace the battered features of his countenance.

The swelling of his eye appeared to be lessening but she knew that the pain must be near unbearable. No one could endure being stabbed and beaten with such savagery and not be in utter agony, regardless of his annoyingly male determination to be brave.

Unable to do anything for the wounds, she reached out to squeeze his fingers, hoping to at least distract him from his pain.

"How did you find me?" she asked softly.

He grimaced as he turned his head so he could meet her worried gaze.

"I was at your home when the lad came to tell me that you had been taken. He was quick-witted enough to follow the hack so I would know where to search."

Simone briefly recalled a grimy-faced lad that had been hovering outside the brewery when she had dashed out to find a weapon to use upon those madmen attacking Gideon. At the time she had barely noted him, but now she realized that the pointed face and overlarge ears had seemed vaguely familiar. As if she had seen him in the streets more than once.

She gave a faint shake of her head. "But how did he know who I am or where I live?"

"It seems that all of London knows of the 'Wicked Temptress,'" he attempted to tease in light tones.

Simone was not so readily convinced that the lad just happened to know who she was, nor that he would risk himself being connected with the villains by going to her house.

Indeed, she was beginning to suspect that the boy was in the employ of Gideon Ravel and was being paid to follow her.

"Mmmm."

His lips twitched at her knowing glance, but it was swiftly followed by a grimace as the carriage hit a stray stone.

"Are you hurt?"

"A few scratches and bruises, but nothing that will not heal. I was more frightened than anything," she wryly admitted.

"Not nearly frightened enough, obviously." The dark gaze suddenly glittered. "When I am recovered we will have a long discussion concerning your foolish behavior. I told you to escape."

She gave a loud sniff, not about to admit that she

would have as soon stabbed herself in the heart as to have left him to the mercy of the scoundrels.

Such a confession would reveal far more than she was ready to admit even to herself.

"You do not give me commands, Mr. Ravel," she told him pertly.

His fingers abruptly squeezed her own with surprising strength. "I will not allow you to be harmed. No matter what the cost."

Her heart gave an odd shudder at his fierce words, but she managed to keep herself from behaving like one of those foolish chits that simpered and purred at every man who cast a glance in their direction.

"Who were those men?" she demanded.

"Wretched souls who have fallen into the power of Mr. Soltern."

"They were . . ." She shivered as she recalled the blank, slack-jawed men who had treated her more as a piece of trash they had picked up off the street than a lady. "I do not know. It was almost as if they were ill."

"Their minds have been destroyed beyond hope."

"Destroyed?" Her breath caught in her throat. "How?"

There was a moment's pause before he at last answered, "Fear."

That was not what he had been about to say, but she was not at all certain that she desired to know the truth.

If Mr. Soltern could do that to men toughened by

the harsh streets of London, what could he possibly do to her?

"Why did they not simply take my necklace if that is what they wanted? I could not have halted them."

"I do not believe it was the necklace they desired."

"Then, what? Money?"

"Perhaps," he replied.

It was a perfectly reasonable deduction, but Simone found herself recalling how easily she managed to slip from the ruffians once Gideon had arrived. They had not so much as called out when she had been bundled out of the door.

"No, not money," she said slowly. "Once you entered the building they made no effort to hold me captive. They were only interested in you."

"Perhaps because I was the one holding the dagger," he suggested in dry tones.

"It was more than that, they were seeking to harm you," she reasoned out loud, her brow furrowed as she recalled the manner the villains had surrounded Gideon. Then suddenly her eyes widened as the truth at last struck her. "That was why I was captured. To lure you to that building. Mr. Soltern wanted you. . . ."

"There is little use in dwelling upon Mr. Soltern's motives," he firmly interrupted. "We are safe."

Simone shivered as she regarded his poor, battered countenance. He had come so horridly close to death.

"Until he decides to try again."

"We shall take greater precautions from now on." The carriage rattled to a halt and he offered her a strained smile. "Ah, I believe we have arrived. My coachman will see you home."

She offered him a frown of outrage at his presumption. "Do not be daft. I am not leaving you."

"Simone." He gave her fingers a warning squeeze. "Wicked temptress or not, you cannot be seen entering a bachelor's establishment without so much as a maid to give you countenance."

She gave an impatient click of her tongue. "You are injured."

"Society will not care."

"Well, I care," she announced in stern tones. "Now, hush so the servants can help you inside."

The dark gaze narrowed at her commanding tone, but at that moment the door was pulled open and Simone hurried out of the carriage so that the servants could help Gideon to the house.

She was not about to leave his side until she was absolutely certain he was properly attended to.

It took surprisingly little effort to negotiate Gideon from the carriage and into the house. In fact, he barely allowed either of the servants to do more than help keep him steady, and Simone gave a disbelieving shake of her head.

She would have sworn he was a breath away from

dying when they had been in the brewery. It seemed amazing he was still conscious, let alone walking.

Entering the foyer, Simone halted as the servants continued up the stairs with Gideon. She knew that he would probably balk at having her present when they undressed him and put him to bed, although she would readily have done the task herself if only to assure herself that his wounds were not as grievous as she had feared.

Impatiently pacing the floor, she waited until she had seen the housekeeper hurrying by with hot water and bandages before she slowly made her way upstairs. Once in the upper corridor she patiently secreted herself behind a large urn until the housekeeper once again appeared, leaving the chamber at the end of the hall, followed closely by the coachman and groom.

Although she was shockingly indifferent to her reputation at the moment, she did not want to wrangle with worried servants over whether or not Gideon was fit to receive her. She was all too aware of how a devoted staff could cluck and stew over their employers.

With silent steps she moved down the corridor to push open the door and slip into the large bedchamber.

For a moment she was halted by the magnificent splendor of the room. With a wide Venetian window that overlooked the garden and walls hung with red and gold embossed leather, it seemed to glow like a jewel in the late afternoon sunlight. Across the room was a black marble chimneypiece and in the very center a gilded, four-poster bed with a red and gold canopy stood in barbaric beauty.

It was exotic, passionate and not at all what she had expected from Gideon.

Gideon.

With a shake of her head at her absurd distraction, Simone hurried toward the bed to discover that he was neatly tucked in the center of the mattress with several pillows stacked behind his head.

"How are you?" she demanded, perching as bold as a tart at the edge of the bed. "Has a doctor been sent for?"

His lips curved with a smile at her anxious tone, and, startling her, he reached out to lightly stroke her cheek with his long, pale fingers.

"I assure you that will not be necessary, my dearest. I will soon be completely recovered."

Her heart warmed at the feel of his tender caress, but she was not about to let arrogant male pride send him to his grave.

"Men," she muttered in annoyance, reaching up to twitch aside the cover so that she could make her own decision upon whether a doctor was in need. "You realize even the slightest wound can become infected. I will decide . . . oh."

Her words stuttered to an abrupt halt as her gaze moved over the smooth, firmly muscled chest that bore no more than angry red welts where he had been stabbed.

In shock she lifted her head to study the cut upon his temple more closely, realizing that it too had faded to a thin scar, while the swelling was nearly gone. He might have been attacked weeks, perhaps months ago.

"I did warn you," he at last broke the stunned silence.

"But . . . this is impossible."

His fingers moved to trace her unsteady lips. "You should really stop using that word, Simone. There are very few things that are impossible."

"Someday you are going to tell me the truth," she whispered in broken tones.

"Someday." The dark eyes probed deep into her own, glittering with an emotion that threatened to steal her very soul. "For now, I need to hold you in my arms and know you are safe."

Simone trembled. To be held in his arms. It was what she wanted more than anything in the world. No, not just wanted. What she desperately needed deep within her.

Somehow, without her even being aware of what was occurring, he had managed to become a necessary part of her world. Every day seemed dull until he appeared. Every night was filled with dreams of being close to him. And despite all the fears and shadows that surrounded him she could not bear the thought that he might someday walk away from her.

But while she might have been foolish enough to allow him into her heart, she still possessed enough common sense to realize that giving in to the passions he had stirred was beyond self-indulgent.

She was supposed to be an experienced widow well versed in the arts of love.

It would take only moments to discover she was a fraud.

Ignoring the regret that viciously stabbed through her, Simone gave a slow shake of her head.

"Gideon, I . . ."

His fingers pressed to her lips as he sensed her reluctant refusal.

"I just wish to hold you, Simone," he said softly. "I need to feel you close."

She hesitated, well aware it was a bad notion in more than one way, but in the end she could as soon have halted the sun from rising as to deny his urgent plea.

"Yes," she whispered, readily settling upon the cover.

With a low groan he reached out to wrap his arms about her and tugged her close. Simone gloried in the feel of his long, hard body as it pressed against her own. Even with the cover between them she could feel the comforting heat reach out to surround her. She breathed deeply of the faint scent of spice that clung to his skin.

All the horror and wretched sense of helplessness slowly faded away as she laid her head upon his chest and listened to the steady beat of his heart.

"Ah, my Simone, this is where you belong," he said in satisfied tones.

Simone closed her eyes as she battled sudden tears.

She had never truly belonged anywhere.

Not with her father, nor her sister and certainly not in that extravagant London town house.

But for the moment she did feel as if she belonged in Gideon's arms.

"Yes."

Chapter 10

Death arrived in Devonshire without warning.

In the sleepy village near the coast the neighbors abruptly began locking their doors at night and eying one another with suspicion. Those forced to leave their homes at night began carrying their firearms and closely watching the shadows for sign of the killer.

There was no explanation for the young women who were being found in their beds with their blood drained from their bodies. Not unless one was willing to believe the unbelievable.

It was all enough to make the most daring of souls begin to peer over their shoulders.

In the small inn next to the town green the local blacksmith and ferryman huddled in a far corner as they enjoyed a pint of ale. There was no one else in the public room excepting the inn keep who morosely watched the empty door. No one wished to leave their homes without dire necessity.

"I be telling you it's the work of a vampire," the ferryman announced in knowing tones as he took a deep sip of the dark ale.

"Get on with you. Are you daft?" the blacksmith growled, his wide, well worn features tight with worry. "T'ain't no such thing as vampires."

"Then how do you explain four young maidens all found in their beds with nary a drop of blood left between them?"

The blacksmith shivered in spite of himself. He was considered a brawny man who had never backed away from a fight, and more often than not was called in when the magistrate was in need of a bit of muscle. These peculiar murders, however, had unnerved even him.

How did one fight a shadow that moved through locked doors and could kill without a sound?

"A madman," he retorted in forceful tones that were meant to convince himself as well as the man seated across the scarred table. "And my bet is upon old Fedmor. I always said as how he wasn't right in the head."

"Fedmor?" The ferryman gave a scoffing laugh. "The poor sod is so in his cups most nights he couldn't find his way to the door. How could he creep about murdering poor innocents without so much as a squeak?"

The blacksmith shifted uneasily. "Then Dalmer. Everyone knows that he's queer in the head."

"And how did he take their blood with only two holes in their necks?"

"Blimey, how am I to know what a madman can do?"

The ferryman suddenly leaned forward, his pale eyes glittering with fearful intensity.

"I'm telling you that we have a vampire on the loose in the neighborhood and I for one intend to take my gels to Salisbury for a nice long visit with their aunt." He gave a shake of his head. "Won't have them becoming fodder for some demon from hell."

The blacksmith took a deep drink of his ale, refusing to give in to the panic that was swiftly turning the villagers into babbling idiots. So far he had halted several young boys who were intent on stoning a feeble old woman, and the father of one of the murdered girls from attacking the vicar.

"Dicked in the nob, you are. Vampires." He gave a loud humph. "Next you'll be telling me we have witches dancing about the maypole."

The ferryman abruptly rose to his feet, his expression one of contempt.

"Stay and die if you like. For me, better a month of Aunt Celia's sharp tongue than dying in me own bed."

Not far from the inn Tristan stroked the hair of the aging servant who knelt at his feet.

It had taken several days to discover the tart, ill-tempered woman who had once been the housekeeper for Lady Gilbert. Not surprisingly, the various relatives who had been landed with the tartar after the Gilbert household had been closed down had done their best to send her as far away as possible.

At last he had managed to track her down to a crumbling cottage near the coast, where she bullied the local children and terrified the vicar.

Putting aside his delight in feasting upon the local maidens, he at last slipped into the cottage and confronted the elderly servant.

Within moments his Inscrollment spell had put an end to her bitter tongue, and she was crawling upon her knees in an effort to please him.

It had still been an effort to at last discover the information that he had sought. Lady Gilbert had been even more clever and treacherous than he thought possible. Indeed, if it had not been for the small miniature that the housekeeper had stolen from the estate to remind her of her mistress, he might never have realized the scandalous ruse.

Now he allowed a pleased smile to touch his lips as the older woman gazed at him with mindless adoration.

"I have pleased you?" she demanded in anxious tones.

He fingered the tiny portrait with his pale fingers. "Oh yes, you have pleased me very much."

"I only desire to serve you."

"Yes, now I believe my work here is done."

"You are leaving?"

"Yes."

She abruptly clutched at the hem of his coat, threatening to wrinkle the superfine fabric.

"Take me with you."

Tristan batted her hands away in annoyance. Really, humans were so tediously weak.

"That is not possible."

Tears openly ran down the wrinkled cheeks as she clutched her hands together.

"No, you cannot leave me. Please."

He slipped the miniature carefully into his pocket before allowing the heat to begin coursing through his blood. He could not leave witnesses to his questioning, despite the fact he had little taste for bitter old women.

He could feel his fangs grow as he thrust his fingers into her hair and jerked her upward.

"Do not fear," he mocked as her eyes widened. "I have a gift for you before I leave."

"What . . ."

Her words came to an abrupt end as Tristan lowered his head and sank his teeth into her neck. Just for a moment her feet kicked in agony, her moans filling the dark, dank cottage. Then just as abruptly she went utterly limp and Tristan tossed her onto the dirt floor.

Removing a dainty lace handkerchief he dabbed at his wet lips. He had what he had been searching for, he acknowledged as the power surged through his body.

Soon Lady Gilbert would be anxious to hand over her Medallion.

And he would be feasting upon her blood.

A pity he had been forced to destroy Gideon before he could appreciate the sight of his lover being drained of her life.

Sending away his valet who had been hovering over him like a mother hen since he had been carried home from the brewery, Gideon set about tying his cravat.

Although it had only been a few hours since the attack, there was no trace of the wounds that had been inflicted by Tristan's servants. His countenance was once again smooth and his chest unmarred by scars.

Still, the horror of discovering Simone at the mercy of those villains remained firmly seared upon his heart.

A fine shiver raced through his body.

If anything had happened to her . . .

"Very nice, Gideon," a rich female voice applauded from the center of the room. "But then, you always were a handsome gentleman."

With a sinuous motion Gideon had pulled the dagger from beneath his coat and whirled to confront the intruder. He froze at the sight of the shabby, gray-haired gypsy who stood regarding him with a mysterious smile.

"Nefri," he breathed, instinctively bowing low in respect. Even from a distance he could feel the power that radiated from her small, bent form and the relentless intelligence that burned in the dark eyes.

"Stop that nonsense," she commanded with a hint of amusement in her tone. Waiting until he had straightened she waved a gnarled hand in the direction of a nearby chair. "Sit down so I do not need to strain my neck to look you in the eye."

Obediently lowering himself into the chair, Gideon regarded her with a faint frown. Even though she was using her powers to alter her appearance, he realized that she would not have revealed herself if the need were not dire.

"What has occurred?" he demanded. "Is it Tristan?"

The old gypsy's lips thinned at the mention of the renegade. "That is one vampire who could use a good strapping," she said in short tones. "He could never be satisfied with what he possessed. Like a child, he always desired what he could not have."

Gideon recalled the deadly mind snare that had been set to trap him.

"He is rather more dangerous than a child."

Nefri gave a slow nod, her expression becoming somber. "Yes, I suppose he is, at that."

"Has he left London?" Gideon demanded, knowing that Nefri would be keeping careful guard on all the traitors.

"For a time. However, he returned before dusk far more dangerous than when he left."

Gideon stilled at the undoubted warning. More dangerous? He had already murdered helpless innocents, had Simone kidnapped and had set a trap for him that had been forbidden for centuries.

How could he possibly be more dangerous?

His features unconsciously tightened with determination. Whatever surprises Tristan had devised, he would not be allowed to harm Simone. Nor to get his greedy hands upon the Medallion. No matter what Gideon had to do to halt him.

"Then I will seek him out and destroy him," he said in even tones.

Nefri regarded him steadily. "He will not allow you to find him until he is prepared. And you must recall that at the moment his powers are greater than your own."

Gideon grimaced with impatience. "I cannot simply wait until he attempts to harm Si . . . Lady Gilbert once again."

A sudden smile touched the lips of the older woman at Gideon's revealing slip of the tongue. A smile that was more than a bit worrisome.

"She is a dear child, is she not?" she demanded in sweetly innocent tones. "But so fragile with the burdens she carries. She needs a strong gentleman she can depend upon when she is forced to confront Tristan."

Although he sensed he was being ruthlessly maneuvered, Gideon did not hesitate in his response.

"I will be at her side."

Surprisingly, Nefri gave a slow shake of her head. "No, I fear you will not."

Gideon stiffened in annoyance. Did the powerful vampire believe that he would fail Simone when she needed him the most? Or that he perhaps feared to face Tristan?

It was unconscionable.

"What do you mean?" he rasped sharply.

"She will not turn to you for assistance if she does not trust you."

With a jerk Gideon was on his feet. Damnation. Nefri had managed to strike at him where he was most vulnerable. Simone did not yet trust him. Even when she had lain in his arms through the long night he had felt the barriers that she kept between them. There were still too many secrets, too many reasons to remain wary of one another.

"I have done all in my power to win her trust," he said defensively.

Nefri gave a slow shake of her head. "You have not yet told her the truth of yourself."

He shoved his fingers through the long hair that he had not yet tied back.

"If I tell her the truth she will be more terrified of me than ever. You know as well as I do how mortals react to the mere mention of vampires. Most do not believe we exist, and those who do consider us monsters."

"Until there is truth between you there can be no trust," she retorted with unshakable logic.

Gideon turned about as his stomach twisted in dread. As much as he disliked the wariness he could sense within Simone, it was far preferable to watching her flee from him in disgust.

She would never understand, he told himself as pain lanced through his heart. The myth of vampires being savage beasts who preyed upon hapless humans was too deeply ingrained. And the very fact that Tristan was ravaging his way through St. Giles would only add to her fear.

If he confessed, he would lose her forever.

He sucked in a sharp breath. He could not bear the loss.

"It is impossible," he said in tortured tones.

"I thought you once said that very little is impossible, Gideon," Nefri lightly teased.

Caught off guard by the realization that the woman had somehow heard the words he had spoken to Simone only last evening, Gideon spun about to confront her, only to discover the room was once again empty.

He released his breath with a loud hiss.

Since coming to London he had hoped that Nefri would seek him out. Not only because she was a legend among vampires, but because he had presumed she could help him to discover some means of luring Tristan back to the Veil without forcing him into a battle.

Now he wished that she had never appeared.

It was obvious she was warning him that he must confess the truth to Simone. And that without her trust he would somehow fail.

The mere thought made a shudder race through his body.

There was a discreet knock on the door before a footman stepped into the room.

"Sir, your carriage is waiting to take you to the boot maker."

Gideon clenched his hands at his sides. Nefri had claimed that Tristan was once again in London. He could not put off the evil hour, no matter how much he might wish to. There was no telling when the desperate traitor might strike.

"There has been a change in my schedule," he said briskly. "Inform the coachman that we will be calling upon Lady Gilbert this morning."

"Very good, sir." With a bow the footman turned to leave the room.

Once alone Gideon reached for a ribbon to tie back his hair.

Only weeks ago he would have scoffed at the mere thought of feeling uneasy at confronting a mortal. He was a vampire. A gentleman far above lesser humans. What did he care if a woman was frightened or horrified by his presence?

His arrogance, however, had been thoroughly punctured by a golden-haired temptress who had managed to capture his heart in a manner he had never before experienced.

He could not lose her, not now.

With a final tug upon his cuffs, Gideon forced himself to leave his chambers.

It was time that Simone discover that the gentleman she had shared a bed with last evening was a creature out of her worst nightmare.

With a practiced skill Simone lightly sketched the outline of a walking dress with a hint of military crispness in the tailored skirt and square neckline.

Putting aside the last of the material she had neatly folded and stacked on the table in the back drawing room, Daisy moved behind Simone and heaved a sigh of appreciation.

"Oh, my lady, 'tis perfect for the dark blue satin," she said.

"Yes, with a touch of gold braiding upon the bodice and sleeves," Simone replied absently, her pencil still moving over the sketchpad.

"It will be lovely."

Simone had to agree. Although she had returned from Gideon's determined to sleep the day through, she had discovered herself far too restless to seek her bed.

Dear heavens, how could she possibly sleep, no matter how weary she might be?

It had been bad enough to be roughly kidnapped by those mindless creatures, and then to fear that Gideon had been murdered before her very eyes. But to have been at his side and watch as his wounds had healed . . .

It should have been terrifying.

She should have fled from his home and refused to ever see him again.

After all, she could no longer deny that Gideon was something other than human.

Instead she had remained, locked in his arms and inwardly wishing that she had the right to remain there for an eternity.

Never had she felt so safe, so utterly at peace.

And it was only the knowledge that her reputation would be in utter ruins if she did not slip away before the servants stirred that had at last sent her scurrying to her own home.

Her fingers trembled and she hastily set aside the pad and pencil.

What was happening to her?

Had Gideon bewitched her? Was she under some mysterious spell that took away all logic and left her vulnerable to emotions she had thought buried long ago?

Her thoughts were still in chaos when the butler stepped into the room and offered a bow.

"Pardon me, my lady, but Mr. Ravel has called."

Simone shakily rose to her feet, briefly considering having him sent away before she dismissed the absurd notion. Gideon had proved time and time again that he would not be halted if he wished to see her.

Besides, if she were to be perfectly honest with herself she could not deny that a part of her wished to be with Gideon. No matter what the mystery that surrounded him, no matter if she felt as if she were going mad.

He had entangled himself in her heart, and she very much feared that she would never be free of her feelings for him.

"Thank you." She somehow forced a smile to her stiff lips. The staff had already developed a great fondness for the gentleman turning her world upside down. There was no use in upsetting them. "Put him in the front salon and tell him I shall be along in a moment."

"Yes, my lady."

Simone briefly glanced down at the deep jade walking gown she had chosen after her bath. It was a lovely gown with an enticing bodice that had stirred more than one admirer to heated glances and indecent proposals.

She wryly wondered if she had chosen the gown knowing that Gideon was bound to put in an appearance.

With a shake of her head at her foolishness, Simone squared her shoulders and forced herself to calmly make her way to the front salon. She might as well try and touch the stars as to comprehend her reactions to Mr. Gideon Ravel.

Entering the large room drenched in morning sunlight, Simone was surprised to find Gideon pacing the carpet as he awaited her arrival.

For a moment she regarded him in silence, drinking in the elegant beauty of his pale features and the chiseled perfection of his male form. With supple grace he moved across the carpet then, no doubt sensing her presence, he turned to regard her with a glittering gaze.

"Good morning, Simone."

Stepping farther into the room she forced herself to assume a casual manner. She would not gape at him as if she were some moonstruck schoolgirl. Even if she did feel like one.

"This is a surprise," she said smoothly. "I did not expect you this morning."

Accustomed to his arrogant self-assurance she was rather startled by the unmistakable nerve that pulsed at the corner of his jaw.

"I must speak with you."

"Very well. Will you have a seat?"

"Not here," he said abruptly. "My carriage is outside. Will you join me for a drive?"

Realizing that something urgent was troubling Gideon, Simone did not even hesitate.

"Of course."

Holding out his arm, Gideon led Simone to the foyer in silence. She swiftly collected a parasol and her gloves before allowing him to steer her out of the house and down the stairs.

Once at the tilbury, Gideon lifted her onto the leather seat and took his place beside her, taking the reins from the coachman.

"I will drive myself," he informed the waiting servants. "You may return home."

With a practiced crack of the whip, Gideon had the grays in motion, and Simone waited with rising impatience as they crawled through the heavy London traffic. She did not know what had occurred, but she did not miss the tension that gripped her companion.

Reluctantly waiting until they had managed to make their way toward the edge of town, she at last gave in to the anxiety that was beginning to form in the pit of her stomach.

"Has something occurred?" she demanded as they turned onto the side path that led to the meadow where they had so recently shared their picnic.

He paused before giving a small nod of his head. "I had a visit from a mutual friend this morning."

Her heart gave an uncomfortable leap. "Mr. Soltern?"

"No. An old gypsy woman."

"Oh." Simone considered his revelation. She had already discovered that the gypsy was acquainted with Gideon, but she had never sensed anything to fear in the old woman. In fact, she had always been oddly at peace when she was in her company. "What did she desire?"

"She has commanded that I tell you the truth of myself," he said in abrupt tones.

Simone stilled, not at all certain she was prepared to hear the truth. Once he spoke the words she realized that there would be no going back to the way her life had been before.

"She commanded you?" she asked, desperate to keep the conversation from coming to its inevitable conclusion.

"When Nefri speaks a wise . . . gentleman listens."

"Nefri? That is her name?"

"Yes."

"And she has some authority over you?"

Gideon gave a strained chuckle. "Over all of us. She is not only powerful, she is a scholar of the ancient arts."

"You . . . you are a gypsy?" she demanded, even as she knew that she was being a fool.

"No." Bringing the horses to a halt, Gideon vaulted to the ground and tied off the reins. Then, rounding the tilbury he helped her to alight. "Shall we take a stroll?"

Hesitating for a moment, Simone at last gave a reluctant nod of her head. Clearly Gideon was determined that she would hear his confession whether she wished to or not.

"Very well."

Pulling her arm through his own he led her across the lovely meadow, his features tight with inner emotion.

"This is very difficult," he at last admitted in low tones. "I do not wish to frighten you."

"Then perhaps it would be best to keep your secrets for now," Simone cowardly urged.

He flashed her a wry smile, as if perfectly aware of her unease. "No, it is too important that you trust me," he said, slowly coming to a halt and grasping her shoulders so that she was forced to face him. "Simone, you must have guessed by now that I am not a mortal."

She was shaking her head even before he finished, her stomach churning with fear.

"No, Gideon, I . . ."

"I am a vampire." He overrode her desperate words with a firm tone.

"What?" The world jerked to a halt as she regarded him in shock. He was mad. Or she was. "No. There is no such thing."

His fingers tightened upon her shoulders as if sensing how close she was to fleeing in anguish.

"They are very real, although we left the world of humans nearly two centuries ago. Now we live in peace behind the Veil. Or at least we did until three renegades fled to London with the intention of destroying our world."

Simone could barely comprehend his words.

A vampire.

They were the stuff of gothic novels and children's

nightmares. Horrifying monsters that sucked the blood of the unwary and lived in the shadows.

They were not handsome, elegant gentlemen who lived in London and stole the hearts of susceptible women.

"No," she whispered in denial.

The dark eyes softened with regret as he regarded her barely restrained panic.

"Simone, there is no reason to fear me. I will not harm you."

She shook her head at his calming words. "I do not believe you. You must be out of your wits."

"Listen to me," he urged softly. "The old gypsy is in fact the most powerful of vampires. Long ago she used an ancient artifact to produce the Veil. When the renegades escaped they came in search of the artifact to bring an end to the Veil and to use the power for their own glory. I was sent to halt them."

Pressing a hand to her stomach she attempted to catch her elusive breath. It helped to assure herself that this was all a terrible dream and that soon she would awaken to discover she was safely tucked in her bed.

"Mr. Soltern?" she demanded in oddly thick tones.

He gave a slow nod of his head. "Yes, he is one of the traitors."

Which, of course, meant that he was also a vampire. Simone shuddered in horror. The man had been in her home. He had touched her.

"And the artifact?"

"It was a Medallion that Nefri wisely divided and offered to three mortal women. She bound them with a spell that ensures that they cannot be taken by force, only freely given."

Simone's hand lifted to the gold amulet that lay against her skin.

"My necklace."

"Yes."

A heavy silence descended as Simone's thoughts whirled through her head too swiftly to follow. It was all so impossible. Vampires and Medallions and strange veils. That did not even include gypsies and traitors.

No sane woman would believe it for a moment.

"You are a vampire," she said in dull tones, as if saying the words would somehow waken her from the wretched dream.

"I fear so."

"And yet you walk in the daylight."

He grimaced at her accusation. "Unlike Tristan I have not taken of human life. The curse of the sun does not affect me."

Against her will her hand shifted to cover her neck. Tristan had taken human life? He had murdered helpless innocents?

Dear heavens, did he intend her to be a victim?

Was that why Gideon had warned her to beware?

Suddenly it was too much for Simone to accept.

Reasonable, sane women did not believe in vampires. Not even when she had seen a picture of Gideon that had been painted three hundred years before, or when he managed to heal wounds that should have put him in his grave.

And she was a reasonable, sane woman, she assured herself.

She was not mad.

"This is not happening," she whispered in broken tones.

"Simone," he frowned with obvious concern. "Are you ill?"

"I wish to return home."

"But . . ."

"Please, Gideon," she pleaded, feeling as if she might shatter to pieces at any moment. "I must have time to consider what you have told me."

He regarded her for a long moment. "What will you do?"

"I do not know." She reluctantly forced herself to meet the dark, compelling gaze. "I truly do not know."

Chapter 11

Tristan waited in the shadows as the frumpy maid neared.

His patience had been severely strained over the past few days.

When he had returned to London he had presumed it would be a simple matter to encounter Lady Gilbert and confront her with his ultimatum. After all, she was always gadding from one social function to another.

But strangely the usually flamboyant widow had cloistered herself in her home and refused to receive even her most devoted admirers.

The gossip had, of course, already started to twitter through town. The less vicious of the Ton implied that she was nursing a heart broken by Mr. Ravel, while others were convinced that she was attempting to conceal the fact that she was carrying his bastard.

Tristan was indifferent to her reason for retreating from society. His only concern was ensuring she realized the danger she faced if she did not give him what he desired.

After dawdling to speak with a local charwoman, the maid at last continued down the street and with silent steps Tristan moved forward to block her path.

"Ah, my lovely damsel in distress," he murmured with a lethal smile. "I do hope you have recovered from your trying experience?"

Giving a small squeak at his abrupt appearance, the maid took a hasty step backward before realizing he was the gentleman who had saved her only a fortnight before.

"Oh, yes sir."

"Good. I should hate to think those wretched men had harmed you."

"Only thanks to you, sir."

"It is always my pleasure to be of help to a lovely maiden," he answered smoothly.

As expected the woman's eyes widened with pleasure. With her plain features and hair more like straw than silk, he did not doubt he was the first gentleman ever to give her such a compliment.

"Lovely? Me?"

"But of course." Glancing down at the basket she carried in her hands, he lifted a silver brow. "Are you returning to Lady Gilbert's?"

"Yes, sir," she readily admitted, unaware that he was carefully steering her in the direction he desired. "I fear she is feeling rather poorly and I nipped out to get a few of those pastries my ma bakes. They are favorites of her ladyship."

"How very thoughtful of you."

"I do not like seeing her so blue deviled."

"No, indeed." Tristan tapped his chin with a thoughtful finger, pretending a concern for the woman he intended to destroy. "I have missed seeing her about as well. Is she ill?"

"A lingering pain in her head."

"Ah, how tedious for her."

"'Tis most unusual. She has always been blessed with a steady constitution. Not at all like most ladies who are forever swooning and taking to their beds."

"She will no doubt be up and about before long." Tristan reached beneath his jacket to pull out a small package he had wrapped in paper. "In the meantime I wonder if you will give her this trifling gift that I purchased for her?"

Annoyingly the maid hesitated as she regarded him with a faint frown.

"Would you not rather give it to her yerself?"

He resisted the urge to knock her to the ground for her impertinence.

"It might be several days before I am able to see her again. I hope this will brighten her spirits."

With clear reluctance the maid took the package he offered. "Very well."

"Do not delay in giving it to her," he commanded in

stern tones. "I am certain it will help to make her forget all about the pain in her head."

"Yes, I will, sir."

He once again flashed his cold smile. "Then be off before those pastries lose their warmth."

Dipping her head the maid scurried past him and headed directly for the large house at the end of the block. Tristan watched her disappear with a surge of satisfaction.

"Soon, my lady," he whispered into the darkness. "Soon you will be in my power and I will sink my teeth deep into you."

Seated at the window seat, Simone stared into the darkness of her garden as she absently shredded a dainty lace handkerchief.

It was the third handkerchief she had destroyed in as many nights.

Not that the destruction was making her feel any better, she acknowledged as she tossed the tattered lace aside. Nor had pacing the floor of her bedchamber for hours on end. Nor even the appalling concoction that had tasted suspiciously of rotting fish that her cook had insisted she drink to help her sleep.

But even as she told herself she was being a fool for virtually making herself a prisoner in her own home, she could not bring herself to step out of her chambers.

How could she possibly face others and pretend that nothing was the matter?

How could she face Gideon?

Or, heaven forbid, Mr. Soltern?

Of its own accord her hand raised to her neck. She still shuddered at the mere memory of Gideon's stark confession.

A vampire?

It was insanity.

Beyond insanity.

And yet, had she not already realized that he was not human? Had she not witnessed his powers?

The light knock upon the door was a welcome distraction, and turning from the window she cleared her worried expression.

"Enter," she called softly, not at all surprised when her maid pushed open the door and crossed the carpet toward her. Poor Daisy had not bothered to hide her growing concern at Simone's uncharacteristic bout of brooding. She had, indeed, taken to arriving in the bedchamber with innumerable treats in the hopes of lifting her mistress's heavy mood. "Daisy, you should be abed."

The kindly maid held out a small basket that offered a most tempting aroma. "I have brought you some of those pastries that you like."

Simone smiled at the young woman who was regarding her with an anxious gaze.

"Thank you. That was very kind of you."

"You must eat something, my lady."

Simone could not halt her faint grimace. Even the thought of food was enough to make her stomach heave in an alarming fashion.

"Yes, I will," she hedged. "Perhaps later."

Daisy gave a disapproving shake of her head, easily able to detect the manner Simone's skin had tightened over the fine bones of her face and the dark circles beneath her eyes.

"'Tisn't good for you to remain in this room and brood. No gentleman is worth becoming ill over."

Simone widened her eyes in surprise at the chiding words. "What makes you believe that I am brooding over a gentleman?"

A knowing expression touched the round face. "If a woman is cast down it can always be blamed upon a gentleman. A right lot of trouble they are."

A near hysterical laugh threatened as Simone thought of Gideon. She could only wish she was annoyed with him because he devoted his time to the gaming tables or had taken a mistress. Those were at least failings she could comprehend.

As it was . . .

She trembled as she instinctively gathered her light robe closer to her body. "True enough. They are trouble I have no need of at the moment."

"Well, as to that, I must say that life would be a

good deal duller without them about," Daisy reluctantly conceded. "They do have their uses."

At the moment Simone would be hard pressed to think of one. Unless she were to count turning her life into chaos and ensuring that she would never again have a decent night's rest.

"I think that I shall go to bed now, Daisy," she said, knowing the maid would remain to prod her into eating the pastries if she did not send her on her way.

The servant turned to leave, then abruptly turned back to regard Simone with an embarrassed expression.

"Oh, I nearly forgot."

"What is it?"

The maid reached into the pocket of her apron to remove a small package.

"A gentleman halted me in the street and requested that I give you this gift."

Simone felt a chill run down her spine as she reluctantly accepted the gift.

"What gentleman?"

Daisy gave a restless shrug. "A rather queer sort, although he did once save my life."

The sense of premonition only deepened at the maid's obvious unease.

"What . . . what did he look like?"

"A large man with cold eyes and long silver hair."

"Mr. Soltern," Simone whispered in horror.

"He seemed quite anxious that you receive this gift as soon as possible."

Simone shivered, longing to toss the package through the window. It was, in fact, what she had done with the priceless bracelet that he had given to her.

Common sense, however, held her hand. Gideon had warned that Mr. Soltern would do whatever necessary to get his hands upon her necklace. She had to discover if he was plotting against her.

"That will be all, Daisy."

The maid dropped a ready curtsy. "Good night, my lady. Just ring if you need me."

"Yes, yes I will."

Waiting until the servant had left the room and firmly closed the door behind her, Simone crossed toward the candle she had left burning on the table beside her bed. Then, sinking onto the side of the mattress she forced her stiff fingers to undo the string tied about the package and peeled back the heavy paper.

A note fluttered onto her lap, but Simone paid it no heed as her heart froze at the sight of the miniature painting that had been revealed.

She recognized it immediately, of course.

It was a portrait her sister had commissioned only weeks before Lord Gilbert's death.

There was no mistaking the glorious golden curls and petulant features, nor the deep rose gown that had possessed golden threads through the bodice.

There was also no mistaking the fact that the portrait had been left in Devonshire since her sister had been quite determined to have a new portrait commissioned with a London artist.

Simone struggled to breathe.

Somehow Mr. Soltern had learned the truth of her past.

A past that was supposed to be buried along with her sister.

Dropping the miniature upon the bed, Simone reached for the note to read the brief message that she was now expecting.

If you do not wish London to know of Sally Jenkins then come to the brewery tonight. Bring the Medallion.

Tristan

Numb with shock, Simone discovered herself rising to her feet and pulling off the robe so that she could don a plain black gown.

What choice did she have, a voice whispered in the back of her mind?

She could not possibly allow him to reveal the truth. Her entire life would be at an end. Dear Lord, she might very well be hauled off to the gallows.

As she dressed, however, her initial flare of horror

began to recede and she forced herself to consider what she was about to do.

It was one thing to face a man intent on extortion.

It was quite another to face a desperate vampire who was willing to murder without remorse.

A ball of ice formed in her stomach at the thought of making her way alone to the brewery and facing Mr. Soltern.

She had always considered herself a courageous and even bold woman. Certainly she could be impulsive. But not even her nerve was equal to this task.

So what was she to do?

Allow Mr. Soltern to destroy her life? Flee London and hope to hide herself in a small village where no one would know her?

But surely the vampire would follow her wherever she would go?

Pacing the floor for nearly an hour, Simone at last came to the inevitable conclusion.

She had to go to Gideon.

No matter how often over the past few days she might have told herself that he must either be a monster or a madman, she knew deep within her that he was the only person in the entire world that she truly trusted.

She might not be able to explain why, but with him she felt safe and cared for in a manner she had never experienced before.

Gideon made her believe that she belonged with him, down to her very soul.

Not giving herself time to consider what she was about to do, Simone silently slipped from her room and made her way to the back stairs.

The night was swiftly passing, she realized with a flare of fear, and there was no telling what Mr. Soltern would do if she failed to show at the brewery.

Remaining in the shadows as much as possible she hurried past the rows of elegant town houses, dodging drunken dandies and the occasional servant as she made her way to Gideon's home. Once there she made her way to the garden and slipped through the narrow door that led to the kitchen.

It was more luck than skill that allowed her to slip silently past the servants who were indulging in a late night dinner and to the back stairs. Thankfully she already knew the way to Gideon's chambers, and with a hasty prayer that she was not about to make a dreadful mistake she hurried down the corridor and pushed open the door to his chambers.

The room was bathed in shadows, but Simone sensed that Gideon was awaiting her as she cautiously inched her way through the darkness. It was in the thick tension she could feel in the air, and the unmistakable sensation of his dark gaze resting upon her.

She stumbled to an uncertain halt, and at that moment a candle flared to life.

Standing beside the vast bed, Gideon was attired in his brocade robe. With an elegant movement he set the candle on a table and moved to take her chilled hands in his own.

"Simone."

"Gideon, I . . ." She briefly faltered, staring at the starkly handsome features that appeared oddly unfamiliar in the flickering candlelight.

As if sensing her wavering nerve, Gideon gently squeezed her hands, a frown marring his brow as he felt the shudder that raced through her body.

"Simone, what has happened?"

"I received a note from Mr. Soltern," she admitted bluntly.

He stilled as his dark gaze narrowed. "What did it say?"

"He demanded that I bring my amulet to the brewery."

"Simone, you cannot allow him to have the Medallion," he said in commanding tones.

She abruptly pulled her hands free and turned from that unnerving gaze. She could not think clearly when he was so near.

"It is not so simple."

"What do you mean?" As she remained silent she heard him step forward and felt the warmth of his hands as he gently stroked them over her shoulders. "Simone?"

She closed her eyes, knowing that the moment had arrived when she must confess the truth. That knowledge, unfortunately, did not make the task any more pleasant.

"You have already surmised that I possess secrets," she said in low tones. "Secrets that I cannot allow others to know."

"Tristan has discovered those secrets?"

"Yes." A sob caught in her throat. "I do not know how, but . . ."

He gently squeezed her shoulders, his breath touching her cheek as he leaned close to her.

"It cannot be so bad, Simone."

"Oh yes. It is very, very bad."

"Tell me, Simone," he urged softly.

Taking a deep breath, Simone slowly turned. Meeting his steady gaze was perhaps the hardest thing she had ever done. She could not bear to think that the esteem he held her in was about to be destroyed. Perhaps forever.

"I am not Simone."

Not surprisingly he regarded her with wary puzzlement. "What?"

"I am Sally Jenkins." The words threatened to stick in her throat and she balled her hands at her sides to keep herself from breaking down completely. "Simone was my half sister, although she would never have acknowledged our connection. I was a bastard, you see."

Oddly there was none of the shock she had expected

to see upon his handsome countenance as he gave a slow nod of his head.

"Your father?"

"Lord Hadwell of Devonshire."

"And your mother?"

"A mere governess of Simone's. She died when I was born."

Without warning his hand reached up to lightly touch her near-white cheek.

"I am sorry."

His obvious sympathy when she had expected anger and recrimination was nearly her undoing and she was forced to bat back the threatening tears.

"It was not so bad while my father lived. He insisted that I be given a home with him and even a measure of schooling with Simone's new governess."

He grimaced as he accurately surmised how her presence in the Hadwell home had been received by Lady Hadwell.

"Which no doubt did nothing to endear you to his wife or daughter."

She could not prevent her shudder at the memory of those wretched years she had spent at the mercy of Lady Hadwell and Simone. No words could express just how evil and vindictive they had been.

"They hated me," she at last said with simple honesty. "Lady Hadwell called me a disgraceful slut and Simone did everything possible to make my life a misery. Even the servants thought my presence an embarrassment to the household. Only my father ever showed me a hint of kindness."

The fingers cupped her cheek. "My poor dear."

Her eyes darkened as she was forced back to those days she had hoped never to recall.

"It only became worse once my father died. I was commanded to become Simone's maid."

His features hardened with anger. "I suppose they hoped to humiliate you."

"Yes." She gave a humorless laugh. They had more than humiliated her. They had stolen every hope she had harbored for a future untainted by their spite. "And when Simone wed Lord Gilbert I was taken to that horrid house where I was not allowed to speak to anyone but my sister."

"Bloody hell," he muttered beneath his breath. "Why did you remain?"

"I had no choice. Simone ensured none of the other servants would help me. And the few occasions I did attempt to flee she made certain I was properly punished."

"What did she do?"

Simone paused. Never before had she revealed what she had endured at her sister's hands. It was astonishingly difficult to force the words past her stiff lips.

"She beat me," she at last managed to admit in harsh tones. "Of course, she beat me for every mistake I made, whether they were real or imagined. But the last occasion . . . an infection set in and I nearly died. In truth, I prayed to die."

His fingers tightened upon her cheek as his gaze darkened to a smoldering ebony.

"Would Lord Gilbert not come to your aid?"

"He was past eighty when they wed and he rarely left his chambers. The only reason Simone wed him was because he was extraordinarily wealthy."

"And close to death?"

"Precisely." Simone's stomach clenched as she recalled her sister's callous anger when the elderly gentleman continued to cling to life day after day. An anger that she regularly vented on her hapless sister. "She hated living in isolation at the estate and less than six months after his funeral she was packed and prepared to travel to London. She was not about to waste an entire year on mourning a gentleman she barely tolerated."

"And you came with her?"

"Yes, she was determined that I would witness her grand debut."

"What happened?"

Simone again hesitated. The trip to London was still a vague fog in her mind. Perhaps because she had no desire to truly ponder what had led to her outrageous charade. Or the undoubted sins that lay heavy on her soul.

She unconsciously wet her dry lips, intensely aware of the dark gaze that watched her every expression.

"We had been upon the road for two days when we were set upon by bandits. They had followed us from the posting inn where we had stayed the night before."

He sucked in a sharp breath at her words. "You were injured?"

"I suffered a blow to the head that knocked me unconscious when we attempted to flee the villains and the carriage overturned in a ditch. When I awoke . . ." Her words broke off and she abruptly buried her face in her hands.

All the horror she had felt when she had managed to drag herself from the carriage rushed back like a physical blow. How many nights had she lain awake recalling the bloody bodies that had been scattered across the road? Even now, months later, it did not seem quite real. More like a persistent nightmare that would not be dismissed.

Moving to place his arms about her, Gideon surrounded her in warm comfort.

"What was it, Simone?"

The strength that he offered her allowed her to slowly raise her head and confront the ghastly memories.

"I . . . I climbed out of the carriage to discover that Simone had been shot along with all the servants. Even her dog had been killed."

"Oh, my sweet," he breathed softly, "you must have been terrified."

"It was horrible. I kept going from body to body

hoping that I was mistaken. I could not believe they were all dead."

He ran a comforting hand down her back, his eyes filled with compassion.

"At least you survived."

"Yes." More than once she had wondered what fickle fate had kept her from being among the bodies on the road. Was it nothing more than blind luck, or had there been some other purpose? A reason she had been spared? "The bandits must have thought I was already dead."

"Thank goodness. They obviously did not intend to leave behind witnesses."

A bleak expression settled upon her pale features. "No. They were very thorough. I lost everyone that I knew in the world on that day."

Chapter 12

Brushing his cheek over Simone's satin hair, Gideon fought back the violent regret that he could not lay his hands upon those who would dare to harm this woman.

The bandits he could punish at his leisure, but her deeper wounds came from the family that should have loved and cared for her.

To think her own sister would beat her, and treat her with such malicious hatred . . .

Bloody hell. It was a testament to her will that she had survived such a brutal and lonely life. And that she had somehow managed to keep her indomitable spirit intact.

"It must have been terrifying to find yourself alone," he said softly, wishing to bring her painful memories to a halt and yet realizing that he must have her complete honesty if he were to protect her from Tristan.

A shiver raced through her body. "I did not know what to do or where to go. I suppose I must have been in shock, but at last I realized I was covered in blood from the bodies." She swallowed heavily. "Absurdly I began ripping off my clothes before I realized that Simone had refused to allow me to bring more than my one gown and a night rail. There was nothing left to do but unpack her trunk and pull on one of her gowns. Do you know, even with her lying there dead I felt terrified at touching her belongings? She would have whipped me unconscious if she had known what I was doing."

His hands tightened on her back, feeling the rough welts that marred her skin even through the material of her gown. His fury rose like bile as he battled to keep his voice calm.

"You were at last rescued?"

She gave a slow nod of her head, keeping her lashes lowered as if unable to meet his gaze.

"Yes, it was several hours later when a coach finally came by and halted to assist me."

"You must have been in a panic by then."

"I believe I must have been out of my mind," she confessed in uneven tones. "That is the only means to explain what happened next."

Pulling back, Gideon gently but firmly tilted her chin upward. Peering deep into her troubled eyes he offered her an encouraging smile.

"You can confide in me, my dear."

She reached out her tongue to wet her lips as she struggled for the courage to continue. Sensitive to her every emotion Gideon silently filled her with his own strength.

"It was a kindly merchant and his wife," she at last continued, her voice so low that only a vampire could have heard her words. "And when they found me alive and in such fine clothing they presumed that I was Lady Gilbert because of the crest upon the carriage."

"I see," he murmured, already suspecting where her story would lead.

"At the time I did not care what they thought as long as I was safe from the bandits."

"Perfectly understandable."

Her eyes grew distant as she was once again caught by her memories.

"They took me to their home and arranged to have the bodies returned to the estate to be buried. When they asked me the names of the servants who had been murdered, I said . . ."

"That the woman was Sally Jenkins, your stepsister?"

"Yes." Her eyes closed as if she feared to watch his reaction to her declaration of guilt. "I knew that no one would bother to even open the coffin for a wretched bastard who was disliked by all. My sister would be buried in an unmarked grave and no one would know she was dead."

"And you would become Simone?"

She gave a reluctant nod of her head as she forced her lashes to lift.

"It is horrid, I know, but the merchant was treating me as if I were a true lady, not some pathetic creature who could expect no more than disdain for having been born." Perhaps unconsciously her hand lifted to grasp his arm, as if seeking to assure him of her sincerity. "Besides which, I had no money and nowhere to go as Sally Jenkins. I would have been forced to the streets unless I could discover a position, which would have been impossible without a reference. More than likely I would have landed in the nearest brothel if I hoped to survive."

His brows drew together at the mere thought of this fragile creature being passed among indifferent males as they took their pleasure with her.

"Never," he retorted, his voice harsh.

She smiled sadly at his obvious outrage. "Some would say it would have been the more admirable choice. Instead I allowed the merchant to continue to believe I was Lady Gilbert and when he offered his carriage to take me to London, I accepted."

For what he knew of humans, he realized that her choice had been astonishingly bold. Surely most maidens would have been far too terrified to travel to a strange city under the guise of a noblewoman?

"A rather daring adventure. What if you were recognized?" he demanded.

"Actually, London was the perfect choice," she confessed with a grimace. “Neither Simone nor I had ever visited the city.”

“But surely there are those who knew your sister?”

She gave a lift of one shoulder. “Very few. We were raised quietly in Devonshire, and after the wedding to Lord Gilbert Simone became as trapped as myself at the estate. Lord Gilbert was too ill to entertain or to travel and Simone thought herself too far above the local neighbors to associate with them. Only the servants and villagers would have known her by sight and they would never leave Devonshire. And in truth, Simone and I look a great deal alike. I believe that was one of the reasons she hated me with such passion. Every time she looked at me she could see herself and she detested the knowledge that a mere bastard could resemble her so closely.”

“Yes, I can imagine,” he said dryly, unable to accept that Simone could ever have been as lovely as this woman. Such a black soul would surely have marred any beauty. “Still, it was a risk to boldly act the part of your sister.”

She gave a short, unsteady laugh. “I have discovered that people see what they wish to see.”

Gideon’s own lips twitched in reluctant amusement. He was quite familiar with the gullibility of humans. Not one had questioned his arrival in London, nor his claim of being connected to European royalty. As long as he looked and acted the part the Ton was satisfied.

“True enough.”

"But now . . ."

Her eyes darkened as she regarded him with desperation. Gideon was abruptly recalled to the reason she had sought him out in the first place.

"Now Tristan has discovered the truth?"

She gave a slow nod of her head. "I do not know how, but he managed to discover a miniature that had been painted of Simone only a month before Lord Gilbert died. He also knows of Sally Jenkins."

"He must have traveled to Devonshire," he murmured, suddenly realizing why the murders had so abruptly halted.

She bit her lip with enough force to draw a drop of blood. It was a revealing gesture of just how distressed she was.

"If he begins spreading gossip that I am not Lady Gilbert the truth is bound to come out. I will be ruined. Perhaps even thrown in prison."

Gideon reluctantly stepped from her trembling body. He needed to concentrate on Tristan's latest gambit. An impossible task when he was close enough to feel the silken heat of Simone surrounding him.

He was far too conscious of the large bed directly behind him, and just how easy it would be to scoop her off her feet and onto the mattress. He did not want to think of the renegade vampire or the danger that surrounded Simone. All he desired was to have her in his arms so that he could reveal the untold depths of his need for her.

With an effort he thrust away the dark desires swirling through his body and turned his thoughts to the traitor who was even now waiting to destroy this woman.

"Nothing will happen to you," he assured her in firm tones.

"But, unless I give him the necklace . . ."

"No," he interrupted sternly. Although he would do anything for this woman, sacrifice his very soul if necessary, he could not allow the Medallion to fall into Tristan's hands. Not only would the vampires suffer from his demented lust for power, but every human would soon discover fear that they never dreamed possible. Besides, he knew that the moment she no longer possessed the Medallion to protect her, Tristan would do just as he promised. Simone would be dead before she could even attempt to flee. "You must trust me. Can you do that?"

There was a long, tension-filled silence before Simone at last gave a nod of her head.

"Yes."

Relief, as sharp as a rapier, flared through him, and without considering his actions, Gideon moved forward to place a soft, lingering kiss upon her lips.

He had waited so long for the barriers to be lowered. And after he had revealed the truth he had very much feared that this moment would never come.

How could she ever trust a gentleman who claimed to be a mythic creature she did not even believe in? Or if she did believe, had been taught to fear?

But there was no mistaking the shimmering certainty in her eyes and Gideon felt the heavy despair that had plagued him for the past three days suddenly being lifted from his heart.

With the hope he could someday teach her to love him as he loved her he knew he could face anyone or anything.

Including Tristan.

Pulling back he ran a hand over the soft satin of her hair.

"Go down to the foyer. I will attire myself and collect the carriage."

"We are going to the brewery?" she demanded.

"Yes. It is time that Tristan and I settle this once and for all."

"I—" Her words broke off as she regarded him with obvious fear.

"What is it, Simone?" he demanded, before abruptly grimacing as he realized he had used her sister's name. "I am sorry. That is simply how I think of you."

Her lips twisted at the irony of becoming the woman she had once hated.

"It is how I think of myself now. It is as if Sally Jenkins never existed. Odd, is it not?"

"No." He smiled deep into her troubled eyes. "You

have become the woman you longed to be using that name."

"But it is not mine."

"You have made it your own," he argued in tones that defied contradiction.

A renegade flare of amusement lightened her taut features at his arrogant assurance.

"I fear others would not share your sentiment."

He shrugged his unconcern. "What do we care for others?"

She reached up to gently touch his cheek, sending a flare of searing heat through him.

"Gideon, you must promise me that you will be careful."

The husky concern in her voice made him tumble into love with her all over again. No one had ever felt the need to worry over his safety. He was, after all, immortal. Not to mention far too arrogant for anyone to believe he was in any way vulnerable.

But astonishingly he discovered he very much liked the thought of this woman fussing over him.

He turned his head to press his lips to the palm of her tiny hand.

"I am always careful."

Her lips thinned at his adamant words. "You may have forgotten the last occasion we were at the brewery, but I assure you that I have not."

He gave a brief nod of his head at her direct hit. He

had stumbled into the brewery blind on the last occasion. This time he would be prepared.

"I will be on guard, I assure you."

Her fingers tightened upon his cheek as her brows knit together.

"I do not believe I could bear anything to happen to you."

He lifted his own hand to cover her chilled fingers. "Nothing is going to happen. I will not allow it. Not now that I have discovered you."

Their gazes entwined as a thick, poignant silence filled the air. Through the bonds that had been woven between them Gideon could feel her pulsing emotions. Fear. Bewilderment. The pain from wounds that had not yet healed. And, through it all was a steady strand of unwavering love that connected her to him as firmly as if they were bound by chains.

"Gideon," she whispered softly.

He stilled, decidedly awed by the sense of fierce satisfaction that filled his heart. She might not yet have admitted to herself that she belonged to him, but he no longer doubted. It shimmered within her with an unmistakable glow.

Taking her fingers he once again pressed a soft kiss to her palm. He wished to be done with Tristan so that he could concentrate fully on this wonderful, maddening woman.

"We will discuss this later," he promised in husky tones. "For now, go down to the foyer and await me."

With a reluctant nod of her head she turned to slip from the room. Gideon paused, forcing himself to take a steadying breath.

For all of his confidence in assuring Simone that all would be well, he was not so foolish as to underestimate Tristan.

Not only did he have the powers of his bloodlust, but he had proven he was willing to use any means, even those forbidden, to achieve his goal. Such desperation made him more dangerous than ever.

That unfamiliar sense of fear returned.

Not for himself. At least not in the physical sense.

But fear that he might fail.

He could not allow that to happen.

If he did . . . the woman he loved would die.

The dark, stench-filled streets of the Rookery seemed uncommonly quiet as they pulled the carriage to a halt.

In the distance the sounds of the gin houses and calls of the prostitutes echoed eerily, but nothing stirred among the decrepit buildings that pressed close to the brewery.

Seated beside Gideon, Simone gave a violent shiver as she peered into the shadows.

"I am afraid," she said softly, not at all embarrassed to admit her building panic.

Reaching out a hand he covered her fists clenched in her lap with a comforting warmth.

"I will not allow Tristan to harm you."

She turned her head to regard him with a troubled gaze. "He is a vampire."

"Yes, and because he has taken human life he is extremely powerful."

Her stomach quivered in horror, for the moment she could not think of the poor victims Tristan had murdered; her concern was only for Gideon and the risk he was about to take.

"More powerful than you?"

"In some regards," he admitted, then, shifting his hand from her own, he reached beneath his coat to remove a small dagger. "I do, however, have a weapon he fears above all others."

Simone was not overly impressed with the dagger. It hardly appeared to be a weapon suitable of disposing of a vampire.

"What will it do?" she demanded in puzzlement.

There was a pause before his elegant features abruptly tightened with distaste.

"It will kill him."

Simone was swift to sense the reluctance in his words. Whatever Tristan had done, he was a vampire and it was obvious that Gideon would take no pleasure in his death.

"You do not wish to use it?" she asked gently.

"No." His gaze shifted to the shabby brewery, a frown marring his brow. "Killing another vampire is like killing a father or brother. I would prefer he return behind the Veil."

"Do you think that likely?"

"No." There was a pause before he abruptly turned to leap from the carriage. Rounding the horses he helped her to alight. "We must wait no longer."

She grasped his arm in a firm grip. "You will remember to be careful?"

He gazed down at her with dark, unreadable eyes. "Yes, but I will have a promise from you before we enter."

There was an edge to his voice that warned her she was not going to like what he was about to demand.

"What is that?"

"If anything happens to me, you are to flee as swiftly as you are able and seek out my cousins. They will protect you."

"I . . ." She swallowed heavily, unable to even consider the possibility that Gideon might be harmed. "Very well."

"Your promise, Simone," he demanded, easily seeing through her attempt to avoid a direct pledge. "You cannot battle Tristan. If he cannot possess the Medallion he will destroy you."

She bit her lip, disliking the thought of running out and leaving Gideon. She had waited her entire life to find someone who made her content to be herself. Someone who did not judge her upon who she was, or care if she possessed unblemished bloodlines. Someone who could love her as Lady Gilbert *or* Sally Jenkins.

Still, she knew he was right.

If he was overtaken by Tristan, she could not possibly face the vampire alone. And while she might not care if she lived or died if Gideon was taken from her, she could not allow the Medallion to fall into the traitor's hands.

She owed Gideon that much.

"I promise," she reluctantly conceded.

"Thank you." Taking her hand he pulled her into the shadows. "This way."

Unable to match Gideon's silent tread, Simone stumbled behind him, coming to a startled halt as he paused before the open door.

Turning, he bent close to her ear. "Tristan is inside. Remember your promise."

Simone battled her rising panic as she gave a slow nod of her head. For all that she had endured in her life, she knew that nothing could prepare her for this. She could only hope that she was strong enough.

Gripping his hand tightly she walked at his side as

they entered the brewery, when there was a sudden flare of light as Tristan lit a lantern. Like Gideon she had already sensed the presence of the vampire, and had no doubt he was well aware of their arrival.

Attired in a bloodred coat and gray pantaloons the vampire might have been just another flamboyant dandy if not for the gaunt hollowness of his countenance and lethal glitter in his eyes. Even in the flickering light there was something unearthly about his presence.

The cold smell of him filled the air, but not completely enough to disguise the wretched stench of a rotting corpse. Simone shuddered, a tangible sense of danger crawling over her skin.

Seeming to flow to the center of the large room, the vampire regarded Simone with a mocking smile.

"Ah, the delicious Lady Gilbert, at last," he purred softly. "And, of course, the ever faithful Gideon."

Gideon gave a slight incline of his head. "Tristan."

"I must say that I am rather surprised at you, Simone," the vampire continued, his awful gaze taking a slow survey of her tense form. "I did not believe you would be willing to confess your rather sordid secret to anyone. You did tell him of your little secret, did you not?"

Attempting to disguise her raging fear, Simone tilted her chin to a defiant angle.

"Yes."

Tristan's lips twisted with ugly amusement, as if fully aware of her inner panic.

"Pretending to be your dead sister, very naughty," he chided. "How do you think the Ton will react when they discover you are no more than a common bastard masquerading as one of your betters?"

Feeling Gideon softly squeeze her fingers in encouragement, Simone shockingly realized that the threat no longer had the power to terrify her. She could face anything, she acknowledged in amazement, even exposure and the inevitable condemnation from society, as long as Gideon was at her side.

"I no longer care," she said in proud tones.

The vampire briefly faltered as his eyes narrowed. "Liar. You will do anything not to be exposed."

She managed to meet his gaze without flinching. "I have already confessed the truth to the one person who matters."

Gideon pulled her closer as Tristan angrily stepped closer, his hands clenched at his sides.

"Do not be a fool, Simone. I will have the Medallion."

With a smooth step Gideon was moving to stand between her and the advancing vampire.

"No, I think not, Tristan."

Peering around Gideon's large form, Simone watched as Tristan swiftly regained command of his temper and returned to his image of mocking nonchalance.

"I am weary of your interference," the vampire drawled, waving a thin hand in dismissal. "Once I have dealt with Lady Gilbert, I will ensure you are properly punished."

"You already failed once to be rid of me," Gideon retorted without the slightest trace of fear.

Without warning the vampire gave a short laugh. "Did you enjoy my little surprise?"

"It convinced me that you must be halted—even if it means I must kill you."

"Fah, what a pathetic wretch you have become, Gideon," Tristan taunted even as his lean form tensed to strike. "Soon this mortal woman will have a leash about your neck so that she can prance you about town like a lapdog. Do you have no pride left?"

Ignoring the deliberate attempt to goad his temper, Gideon faced his adversary squarely.

"Will you return to the Veil?"

"Never," Tristan spat in disgust.

"Then it appears we have nothing left to discuss."

Tristan shrugged, his smile intact as he watched Gideon slowly move toward him.

"You know, I did hope to leave you alive long enough to watch as I enjoyed the blood of your lover. But perhaps once I have you in my command, little Sally will realize she has no choice but to give me the Medallion."

"It is over, Tristan," Gideon warned.

"For you."

With a movement too swift for Simone to follow Tristan struck out, knocking Gideon to the ground. She cried out, but even as she stepped forward, Gideon was back on his feet with the dagger firmly in his hand.

The two slowly began to circle one another, both warily waiting for the other to strike. Simone pressed a hand to her mouth, anxious not to distract Gideon for even a moment.

They continued to circle, then without warning Tristan simply vanished in a wisp of fog, just as abruptly appearing behind Gideon and slamming his hands into the back of his head.

Gideon staggered but swiftly turned to face the vampire.

Tristan flowed backward, careful to avoid the dagger, his lips pulled into a vicious smile.

"What is it you want, Gideon?" he demanded. "A share in the power?"

"I have no desire for power, Tristan. I only wish to protect the Veil."

The mist again swallowed Tristan and to her horror, Simone watched as a deep cut appeared on Gideon's cheek.

"Show yourself, you coward," Gideon snapped, suddenly shifting as the mist gathered behind him and more blood began to pour from a cut on his back.

"Join me, Gideon," a disembodied voice whispered. "Together we could rule the world."

"Your thirst for power has driven you mad," Gideon retorted, fluidly turning to watch as Tristan again reappeared. "You would sacrifice us all for your own glory."

"But of course." The vampire laughed in a scornful manner. "My glory is all that concerns me."

"It will not be allowed," Gideon warned, his hand clenched tight upon the dagger in his hand.

Across the room Simone could feel his sharp emotions. As much as he might detest what the vampire had become in his frenzy for power, he still wavered in using the dagger. He could as easily have plunged the weapon in his own heart.

No doubt aware of Gideon's reluctance, Tristan gave a dismissive wave of his hand.

"There is no one who can halt me. Not even Nefri."

Gideon surged forward, but as swiftly as he moved he was not quick enough. In the blink of an eye, Tristan was gone and suddenly Simone felt the deadly cold clutch of his fingers as they clutched about her neck. Shock held her still as Tristan tightened his grip and she felt the air being squeezed from her body.

"No," Gideon cried.

"Tell her to give me the Medallion, Gideon," he warned in icy tones.Simone desperately sought to breathe, her eyes wide with fright even as she gave a faint shake of her head.

"Let her go," Gideon commanded, his face set in lines of deadly determination.

"Only after she has given me what I desire."

"Tristan . . ."

"She is dying. I can feel her life slipping away. Now tell her to give me the Medallion," Tristan growled, giving Simone a shake.

"No."

Fighting the darkness that threatened to consume her, Simone watched Gideon abruptly straighten. Behind her Tristan tensed, prepared to battle a sudden attack. But just as Simone realized that Gideon would never reach her before Tristan could snap her neck, there was a blur of movement and a shocked gasp of disbelief from behind her.

The hand about her neck fell away and stumbling to her knees, Simone shifted about to see Tristan lying on the hard floor with the dagger deeply plunged into his heart.

Still panting with the effort of trying to breathe through her bruised throat, Simone felt Gideon come to kneel beside her. Her gaze, however, remained upon the body next to her.

In horror she watched a shimmering glow outline the long form, flickering in the dim light, then appallingly the body began to turn to ash. Her eyes widened as Tristan simply crumbled onto the floor until there was nothing left but the faintest trace of darkness upon the stone.

A comforting arm encircled her trembling body and Gideon pressed a kiss to her temple.

"It is done."

Chapter 13

For a moment Gideon simply held on to Simone, allowing the warmth of her to seep into his chilled heart.

He had not realized how difficult it would be to kill Tristan. Not even when he had known that his own life was held in the balance could he force himself to plunge the dagger into the traitor. To bring the life of a vampire to an end went against every moral he possessed.

It was not until Tristan had dared to threaten Simone that his revulsion had been thrust aside and he had reacted without even thinking.

Now, however, reaction was setting in and he shivered in disgust.

Not only at having killed, but the knowledge that he had very nearly waited too long.

One more moment and Simone would be dead.

And he would have been entirely to blame.

His arms tightened about her, his lips unable to stop stroking the satin skin of her temple. He had to reassure himself that she was alive and in his embrace where she belonged.

"Simone, are you harmed?" he demanded in rasping tones.

He felt her shiver as she leaned against him. "Nothing that will not heal."

"Damnation," he cursed his weakness at the sound of her strained voice. It was obvious her throat had been injured. "I was terrified Tristan would kill you before I could reach you. I had no choice but to throw the dagger and hope for the best."

Her fingers rose to touch the amulet that lay upon her skin. "He was too determined to have the Medallion," she husked.

Gideon gave a slow nod of his head. He was well aware that it had been Tristan's obsession for the Medallion that had made him hesitate in striking Simone down.

He could only thank Nefri that he had paused.

"Yes. It was his downfall. That and his confidence that I would not choose to destroy him. I very nearly waited too long."

Easily able to sense his inner turmoil, Simone raised her hand to gently lay it against his cheek.

"Gideon, do not."

His lips thinned. "I allowed him to hurt you."

"You attempted to give him an opportunity to save himself," she argued in soft, but ruthless tones. "Had you simply killed him without remorse or regret you would be no better than he."

Her words, of course, made sense, but he was not yet prepared to accept what he had done.

"He had become crazed with his lust for the Medallion."

Simone slowly turned her head to regard the darkened stones. "What happened to him?"

With reluctance, Gideon reached out to retrieve the dagger that lay on the ground.

"The power of the blade destroyed his soul."

Her breath caught. "His soul?"

"It is as if he never existed. A horrible fate for any vampire."

As if at last truly comprehending just how final a death Tristan had suffered, Simone regarded him with sad eyes.

"I am sorry, Gideon."

"As am I." He briefly thought of his arrogant certainty when he had arrived in London. He had never thought that Tristan would prove so relentless. It had seemed a simple matter to convince him of the error of his ways, and to escort him to the Great Council. "I did not believe it would come to this."

There was a faint pause as Simone studied his tortured expression.

"Why were you sent to face him?" she at last demanded. "Surely there were others more capable?"

His pride was ridiculously pricked by her abrupt question. Did she feel as if he had somehow failed her?

"More capable?"

"I presume that vampires can be as different from one another as humans are. There must have been another who would not have been so reluctant to face Tristan."

He frowned at her perception, for the first time actually pondering the reason he had been called before the Great Council. It was true that there were those who would have been quite anxious to punish the renegades. Some far more talented in the arts of battle than he.

"I do not know," he slowly confessed. "At the time I was told I had been chosen I presumed that it was because I was intelligent and always logical. Now . . ."

"What is it?"

A niggling unease settled in the pit of his stomach. He knew that he must be overlooking something. Some vague sense that there was more to this than he could put his finger upon.

"It does not make sense," he muttered in annoyance for his uncommon stupidity. "As you say, there were others that surely would have been far more capable of facing Tristan."

Her expression abruptly melted as she gazed deep into his eyes. "Whatever the reason, I owe them a debt of gratitude. I would not have desired anyone but you to protect me."

Gideon readily allowed himself to be distracted, and slipping the dagger beneath his coat he firmly returned his arms about her delicious form.

"No one else will ever be allowed to protect you. You belong to me."

She arched her brows at his deliberately arrogant tone. "Belong?"

He breathed in her warm scent. "Can you not feel it deep within you?"

Her eyes briefly closed before they opened to regard him with shimmering love.

"Yes."

Gideon gave a low groan as he pressed his lips to her forehead. The last three days had been the longest in his life as he waited for her to come to him. He'd wanted so desperately to force his way into her home where he could prove to her that his emotions were no different than any other gentleman's. And that he would devote his life to making her happy.

Only the knowledge that he might very well force her even farther from him had kept him away.

"I thought I had driven you away when I confessed the truth."

"It was difficult to accept," she admitted.

"Yes, I know."

She heaved a faint sigh. "I wanted to convince myself that you were mad and that my feelings for you had been those for a gentleman who did not exist."

"But you came to me tonight."

"I realized that there was no one else that I could trust," she said simply.

He pulled back to study her pale features. It was past time for honesty between the two of them.

"Because of your secrets?" he demanded gently.

"In part. I thought . . ." She gave a wry smile. "Rather, I hoped that you would not turn from me in disgust when you learned my true identity."

He gave an impatient click of his tongue, still amazed that she would think for a moment that he could care about such a trivial matter.

"I would never turn from you," he assured her. "Certainly not because your mother was not of noble blood. Such things mean nothing to me."

Her eyes darkened with sudden emotion. "That is only a measure of why I came to you tonight."

"Tell me why, Simone," he urged.

"Because I could no longer deny that I had fallen in love with you."

Sweet, heated pleasure rushed through Gideon as he allowed her words to sink deep within him. He never thought to feel this way, nor to depend upon another to bring him such happiness.

"Oh, my sweet, you fill my heart with joy," he groaned softly.

Shifting awkwardly on the hard floor to place her arms around his neck she offered him a wry smile.

"I can think of more comfortable surroundings to continue this conversation."

Gideon gave a rueful chuckle. He had been so enwrapped in Simone he had nearly forgotten the dreadful brewery.

"True enough." Rising to his feet he carefully helped her to stand, assuring himself that she was not still suffering from her ordeal before slipping her arm through his own and leading her toward the door. Watching her carefully he did not miss her grimace as they moved through the flickering shadows. "What is it?" he demanded in concern.

"That horrible smell."

Gideon's features tightened, wishing that he could protect her from the truth.

"It is no doubt Tristan's servants."

She lifted her head in surprise. "He killed them?"

"No, but once they became trapped in his power they would no longer be concerned for their own needs. Most starve to death within a few days."

She shuddered in disgust. "How horrid."

"Yes."

They walked in silence out of the brewery and into the alley before she inevitably realized how helpless she could have been in Tristan's power.

"Dear heavens, why did he not do the same to me? I would no doubt have given him the Medallion without question."

He placed his arm about her shoulder at the edge of fear in her voice. "Because the Medallion itself protects you. Not even I was able to use Compulsion to sway you to my will, although my talent is far greater than Tristan's. It caused me no end of annoyance."

Thankfully his teasing words lightened her dark expression and she flashed him a speaking gaze.

"Then I am not under some mysterious spell?"

Gideon paused to help her into the carriage before taking his own place and urging the horses down the street.

"Only the spell of my irresistible charm," he assured her with a roguish grin.

She gave a loud sniff at his arrogance. "I would not claim it irresistible."

He arched a dark brow. "You dare to question the power of my charm? Obviously I shall have to prove to you just how irresistible I can be."

A smile touched Simone's lips as they swiftly made their way back toward the more fashionable streets of London.

It was over.

Truly over.

Tristan could no longer threaten her, and most important of all, Gideon was safe.

It seemed unbelievable.

There would be no more glancing over her shoulder in fear that she was being followed, no more nights haunted by dreams of the vampire, no more pacing the floor in fear that Gideon would be taken from her.

Gideon.

Her smile slowly faded as she glanced at the purity of his handsome profile.

She had been so concerned that something might happen to him, that she had never taken the time to consider what would happen once this was all over.

Tristan was dead. There was no more threat to her. And no more reason for him to remain.

Whatever his claims to possess feelings for her, his place was not in London. And she could not go with him to the mysterious Veil.

A hollow emptiness filled her even as she struggled to hold on to her composure.

She would not make this difficult for Gideon, she swore to herself. He had given her too much to make him feel guilty for what he must do.

She would simply live for the moment and accept whatever he could offer.

Distracted by her dark thoughts, Simone paid little heed to their progress through town until the carriage came to a halt and she realized that they were in the mews behind Gideon's home.

A renegade flare of excitement flared through her as she realized that their time together was to be prolonged.

Whatever he offered, she told herself, ignoring the

tiny voice in the back of her mind that chided her scandalous behavior.

"You are very certain of your charms to bring me to your home at such an hour," she attempted to tease in light tones.

"No." He turned to regard her with a somber expression. "I just cannot bear to allow you out of my sight. I came far too close to losing you tonight."

Her heart leaped at his words. "Oh."

"Will you join me?"

She hesitated only a moment before giving a nod of her head. She might later regret her reckless behavior, but for now she needed to be with Gideon.

"If you wish."

"With all my heart," he murmured softly.

For a moment they gazed at one another in silence, then as a sleepy groom slowly shuffled toward the carriage, Gideon swiftly leaped down and moved to swing her to the ground.

In silence they moved toward the darkened house, using the same path she had used earlier to enter the kitchen and up the back stairs. It was not until they were in Gideon's chamber and he was lighting a candle that her nerves at last made themselves known.

Pacing uneasily toward the window she cleared her throat. "It will soon be morning."

"We have a few hours yet," he murmured.

She turned to discover him regarding her with a watchful gaze.

"A few hours for what?" The words burst out before she could halt them.

He slowly smiled as he held out his hand. "Come, Simone."

Gathering her courage Simone moved toward him, even allowing him to lead her to the large bed so that they could perch upon the edge of the mattress.

Uncertain what was to come next she was startled when he made no motion to touch her beyond stroking a hand softly over her hair.

"What is it, Gideon?" she demanded, wondering if she was supposed to do something.

"You have told me that you love me."

"Yes."

His fingers moved to touch her cheek. "Already we share much of each other. You can sense when I am near and what I am feeling."

Her eyes widened in shock at his words. "How did you know?"

"You are just as deeply branded within me."

She gave a slow shake of her head. She had barely allowed herself to acknowledge just how aware she was of Gideon. Not only the sense when he was near, but the unmistakable realization that his emotions were irrevocably enwrapped with her own.

"It is so strange. I have never experienced this before."

He smiled at her wondering tone. "It is a gift known only to vampires."

"But I am not a vampire," she ridiculously retorted.

"No, but you wear a powerful artifact of my people. It has already altered you in many ways."

Simone's hand instinctively rose to touch the golden amulet. It was true that she had noted the subtle changes in herself. Her heightened senses and even being able to see more clearly in the dark. It was not precisely frightening, but, to actually consider that she was being altered . . .

"Good heavens," she breathed.

"Do not fear," he gently comforted, those distracting fingers continuing to send pleasurable tingles through her body. "It will not harm you."

"No, I suppose not."

He paused before he tilted her chin upward so that she was forced to meet his searching gaze. "Simone?"

"Yes?"

"Do you trust me?" he demanded.

She blinked at the odd question. "You know that I do."

"Enough to place your future in my hands?"

The very air seemed to thicken with tension as she studied his pale features. Was it possible that he did not intend to leave her? That he would remain in London with her?

It was what she desired more than anything in the

world, but she was frightened to allow her hopes to be raised.

"Are . . . are you asking me to wed you, Gideon?" she asked in cautious tones.

He frowned, as if he were startled by her question. "Of course I intend to wed you," he retorted, seemingly unaware that he had just made her dearest dream come true. "But what I ask of you is to join your very soul with my own."

Simone attempted to think through the cloud of joy that filled her thoughts.

He wanted to marry her.

Her.

Sally Jenkins.

Not Lady Gilbert. Not the "Wicked Temptress."

But the insignificant daughter of a governess.

It did not seem possible.

But even as she grew dizzy from shocked delight, she realized he was awaiting her response.

What had he said?

Join their souls?

She gave a faint frown as she attempted to consider what he might possibly mean.

"Is that possible?"

"Yes, but it would mean that we are truly a part of one another." He gently cupped her face in his hands, his dark eyes boring deep into her own. "Our thoughts, our emotions, the very beat of our hearts. We would be bonded for all eternity."

She carefully considered his words, knowing that this was far more important to Gideon than any marriage ceremony.

The thought of being so closely connected with the man she loved did not frighten her. She very much desired to be one with him. But something in his words made her hesitate.

For all that she had accepted who he was, she could not forget that they were very different. As a vampire he was immortal. What would happen to him when she eventually died?

"Gideon, I do not have an eternity," she reminded him sadly.

His hands tightened upon her face. "Who is to say? With the Medallion anything is possible."

She gave a reluctant laugh at his familiar words. "You are very fond of telling me that."

"Because it is the truth." His expression softened with a longing that tugged at her heart. "Simone, I wish to have you as my true mate. Will you?"

She could have denied him nothing at that moment. All the love and need she had tried to deny for so long flooded through her as she gave a nod of her head.

"What must I do?"

"Nothing but trust me," he said in low tones.

She met his gaze squarely. "I do."

Moving slowly, as if afraid that he might startle her into flight, Gideon lowered his hands so that he could sweep her long curls over her shoulders. Then just as slowly he lowered his head, angling it so that he could approach the bare skin of her neck.

Just for a moment Simone instinctively tensed, unsure what was about to happen. The satin blackness of his hair brushed her chin, the scent of spices filling her senses. Of their own accord her hands raised to grasp his shoulders.

She felt the warm brush of his breath upon her skin, then shockingly the sharp points of his fangs.

Panic threatened to rise as there was the faintest prick upon her neck, but before she could give in to fear a warm rush of sensation relaxed her taut muscles.

There was no pain, just the sense of being enfolded in a comforting embrace. Her head tilted backward, allowing him to gently taste of her blood.

It lasted only a moment before he offered a lingering kiss and pulled away.

He did not speak, however, and holding her bemused gaze he lifted his hand and turning it over he bit the inner skin of his wrist. Blood instantly welled and he lifted it to softly place it against her lips.

Startled, Simone instinctively dipped out her tongue to taste of the wetness staining her lips.

She was not certain what she had expected, but it was not the sudden shock of emotions that tumbled through her. Her head spun as she squeezed her eyes shut, attempting to steady herself against the onslaught.

For long moments she struggled to calm herself. She was dazed and not at all certain she could bear the shimmering sensations that threatened to consume her.

Then slowly the torrent began to subside and she was able to concentrate upon the changes within her.

There was the awareness of Gideon, of course. But it was no longer the vague knowledge that he was near. He was clearly nestled within her mind, as well as the sharp sense of concern that held him tightly gripped as he watched her. More than anything, however, she felt the steady, undeniable beauty of his love.

A smile of wonder curved her lips. "Oh."

"Simone, are you . . . well?" he husked, his hands tightly gripping her own.

"I am . . . whole," she said, still marveling at the knowledge that they were truly bound together. "I did not realize how lonely I have been all my life. Now I am complete."

"My sweet." He reached down to delicately touch his lips to her own. "We will be wed according to human custom. I have already procurred a special license."

"You . . . you will not return to the Veil?" she forced herself to ask the question that refused to be dismissed no matter how irrational. Her father had loved her, but he had abandoned her. She could not bear it again.

He easily knew how important his answer was to her.

"Perhaps for the occasional visit, but my place now is with you."

"Yes," she whispered, boldly leaning forward to claim his mouth with her own.

It was the first time she had ever initiated such an intimate caress and she discovered a heady delight as she felt his instant response. Encouraged by the sudden tension that gripped his body, she daringly raised her arms to twine them about his neck, tugging the ribbon from his hair so that she could thrust her fingers into the satin strands.

Gideon gave a throaty growl as his arms wrapped about her, taking firm command as his tongue urged her lips to open.

Simone readily complied, allowing him to deepen the kiss as his hands ran an impatient path over her back. Urgent pleasure flared through her, making her arch toward his warm body with aching need.

The sensation of his own rising passion swirled through her body, heating her blood and making her heart pound. It was astonishingly erotic to have his emotions pulsing through her, and Simone gave a low groan as she impatiently pressed herself closer.

"Simone." With a heartfelt moan he reluctantly pulled back to regard her with a tight expression. "I think I should warn you that if you continue in this manner you will never be returned to your bed."

She allowed a wicked grin to curve her lips. "That was my intention."

"Wench," he chided with a glint of amusement. "If you only knew how long I have ached to possess you."

His teasing words abruptly forced Simone to realize that she had not yet been entirely truthful. She grimaced as she forced herself to pull away from his warm grasp.

After all the lies and charades between them, she had to ensure that when they came together it was in complete honesty.

"I could not give in to my desire no matter how much I might have wished to," she confessed in low tones. "My charade as a widow would have come to a swift end."

He stilled as he considered her confession. "Because you are innocent?"

"Yes."

There was a long pause before Gideon abruptly heaved a deep sigh.

"Ah, my love, you do not know how you torture me."

She frowned at his odd reaction. She had thought that he would be pleased that no other man had ever known her in an intimate manner.

"Torture?"

His hand rose to cup her chin. "We will wait for our wedding night."

"But . . ."

"It is how you have always dreamed it would be, is it not?" he demanded softly.

It was impossible to lie. Her every thought was now open to him. He already knew that even through all the years of torture and degradation she had dreamed that someday she would be rescued by her knight in shining armor.

More often than not it had been a foolish dream. What knight would possibly desire a bastard without a farthing to her name? She was a drudge without friend or even family who would acknowledge her.

And yet, through it all she had battled to maintain her innocence.

Her dream would not be stolen. And when her knight came she wanted to at least give him the gift of her virginity.

Now she was fiercely proud that she could give her innocence to Gideon.

"Yes," she at last admitted with a small smile.

Although she could feel the dreadful struggle it took to rein in his smoldering passions, Gideon merely gave an understanding nod of his head.

"Then that is how it will be. You are already mine in all the ways that truly matter."

Wondering if her heart could burst from sheer happiness, Simone lifted her hand to touch his lips.

"I love you."

Chapter 14

Late the next morning Gideon was seated beside Simone on the bench in her garden. Rather ruefully he patted the special license that was safely tucked beneath his jacket.

When he had agreed to wait for Simone he had imagined they would be wed within a few days, if not hours, but as he came to study the unexpected vulnerabilities of the woman he loved he realized that she deserved more than a hurried marriage before the vicar.

All her life she had been taught to be ashamed of who she was. And while she still maintained her sister's name, he was not about to allow her to think he wanted to hide their wedding from the world.

With considerable sacrifice he had ordered his staff to begin preparations for a lavish ceremony in St. George's Square that would include the entire Ton.

If neither of them were quite whom society presumed them to be it did not matter.

Simone would have her day to shine brightly and he would at last have her at his side.

And just as importantly, a dark voice whispered in the back of his mind, in his bed.

Shifting uncomfortably as his body stirred in anticipation, Gideon choked back a groan of frustration. For all his logic, there was no controlling the endless need he felt for this woman.

Perfectly aware of his scandalous thoughts, Simone glanced up to flash him a wicked smile. The minx was becoming quite adept at driving him mad.

"Well?" she said in those sultry tones that made his blood heat to a near boiling point.

"Well what?" he demanded as he considered dragging her into his arms and reducing her to his own state of discomfort.

She held up the sketch she had been diligently working on for the past few hours.

"It is my wedding gown."

Gideon obligingly studied the smooth charcoal lines drawn upon the pad then gave a decisive shake of his head.

"Absolutely not."

She blinked in surprise at his firm tones. "But it is lovely."

"It may be lovely but there are far too many buttons."

"What?"

Taking the sketch pad from her hands he tossed it onto the bench and roughly drew her into his arms.

"I have waited too long for you. I will not devote half the evening attempting to wrestle you out of your gown."

"Really, Gideon," she attempted to chastise only to give a laugh as he planted desperate kisses down the length of her neck.

"One ribbon," he conceded, continuing the fascinating discovery of the satin skin of her throat. "Perhaps two."

Her hands lifted to clutch at his shoulders, her heart racing in a gratifying manner.

"I see you are to be a tyrant," she complained in unsteady tones.

"Only when it comes to buttons," he assured her, his tongue reaching out to lightly taste of her. "I wish to bed my wife without battling folderols."

"Mmm." Her head obligingly tipped back to allow him access to the vast amount of skin exposed by her plunging neckline. "Ribbons, then. Definitely ribbons."

His mouth sought ever lower, pausing over the rapid beat of her heart.

"I knew you would be a sensible wife."

"How very charming."

The unexpected sound of a voice in the center of the garden had both Gideon and Simone jerking apart in surprise. With lethal swiftness he was on his feet and facing the intruder.

Only when he noted the old gypsy woman smiling in an oddly contented fashion did he relax his guard.

"Nefri," he murmured, offering the powerful vampire a bow as he felt Simone rise to her feet to stand beside him.

"Good morning, Gideon, Lady Gilbert." She moved slowly forward, her numerous bracelets and necklaces jangling with every step. "I see all went well last evening."

Gideon grimaced, knowing it would take some time to heal the wound of Tristan's death. For now he still battled the wretched sense of waste.

"No, not well," he corrected in harsh tones. "Tristan has been destroyed."

Nefri gave a slow nod of her head, her expression one of regret, but with no surprise at his revelation.

"Unfortunate, but I feared it would come to such a fate."

"He was obsessed beyond reason," Gideon agreed.

"Yes." Nefri paused, a thoughtful air settling about her. "And oddly certain he would succeed."

Gideon swiftly followed her unspoken implication. It echoed precisely the unease he had felt last evening.

"Such a thought struck me as well." His gaze narrowed. "How do Sebastian and Lucien go on?"

Nefri's smile abruptly returned, more mysterious than ever.

"Well enough."

"Will they need my assistance?" he demanded, feeling Simone stiffen at his side but knowing he could not allow his friends to suffer even if it meant endangering himself.

Nefri gave a sudden chuckle. "I do not believe they would appreciate interference."

Considering the two vampires who were every inch as arrogant as he, Gideon gave a wry smile. He would have been offended had either attempted to press their assistance upon him.

"No, I do not suppose they would."

The vampire tilted her head to one side, eying him in an intent manner.

"I might, however, call upon you later."

Gideon stilled at her words. Nefri would not seek his help if it were not out of dire need.

"You expect further troubles?"

She paused before giving an irritated shake of her head. "There is more to this than I fully understand at the moment. It is quite vexing."

"I will, of course, come whenever you have need," he promised.

"Thank you." Abruptly turning her head Nefri regarded the silent Simone with a searching gaze. "My dear, you have my gratitude. You have been forced to face great danger to help us."

Surprisingly Simone flushed with embarrassment at the vampire's sincere appreciation.

"I am only relieved that it is all over," she murmured, clearly uncertain how to behave toward the older woman.

"Not truly over, I fear," Nefri softly warned. "You remain the guardian of the Medallion."

Simone's hand rose to touch the amulet at her neck. "Yes."

Nefri's smile once again reappeared. "I believe, however, that the gifts you will receive from the artifact will be worth any sacrifice you might be required to make."

Concerned that the vampire's words might once again frighten Simone with the thought of wearing the Medallion, Gideon turned his head to discover her watching him with love shining in her eyes.

"It has already given me more than I ever dared hope for."

"So I can see," Nefri murmured with obvious amusement. Then, when it became evident that Simone and Gideon were lost in one another, she discreetly waved her hand toward them in a practiced manner. "Be well and happy," she murmured as she blessed their union and silently disappeared.

It was the loud squeak from the hedges that forced Gideon to turn his fascinated attention from the woman at his side, and abruptly shifting he discovered a young scamp running toward him full speed.

"Cor, did you see her?" the urchin demanded as he skidded to a halt directly before Gideon. "She disappeared. Right before me very eyes."

"What the devil are you doing here?" Gideon demanded, his hands planted on his hips.

Unrepentant the lad scrubbed the end of his nose as he conjured his most engaging grin.

"Well, you did say as to watch the lady."

He heard Simone's sniff of disapproval but his gaze never wavered from the thin, grimy face.

"Not when I am here."

"Not ever," Simone intruded, her eyes flashing in a dangerous manner.

"Now, my sweet, they did help me to find you when you had been kidnapped," he argued in reasonable tones.

"That's right. And frightened off more than one persistent nob what wanted to try to slip in without alerting the servants," the lad added in proud tones.

Simone's eyes widened. "What?"

The urchin shrugged with an air of worldly wisdom. "There are always gents that hope to catch a lady unawares like. Disgusting buggers, if you ask me."

"Good heavens," she breathed in shock.

Gideon placed an arm about her shoulders, knowing he would soon be paying a call upon the mysterious nobs. They would soon learn the dangers of even glancing in Simone's direction.

"So you see, me services are invaluable," the lad prompted with a cheeky grin.

Gideon could not help but chuckle at the boy's audacity. "He does make sense, my sweet."

Simone regarded him with raised brows. "I will not allow young boys to spy upon me. For one thing they could be hurt."

"Fah. 'Tis a great deal safer here than on the streets," the boy hurriedly pointed out.

"No," Simone retorted in firm tones. Then, as the boy's face crumpled with disappointment she heaved a sigh. "I suppose I could use a page boy," she reluctantly conceded.

The urchin wrinkled his nose. "A page boy? I would have to stay inside and wear a uniform?"

"Yes," Gideon told him, his own expression firm. "And no stealing."

"Cor, you drive a hard bargain, guv," the lad complained.

"Take it or not," Gideon retorted in tones that defied argument.

"Can I bring the others?"

Simone stepped forward. "Others? How many others?"

The urchin gave a piercing whistle and without warning half a dozen boys, just as grubby as the first, tumbled from the hedges.

Gideon tilted back his head to laugh with rich amusement. He only halted when Simone sharply thrust her elbow into his side.

"Well, you did ask," he told her in unsteady tones.

She glared at him in exasperation. "This is all your fault. What are we to do with six boys from the street?"

"We could always send them back to the stews," he suggested.

She tossed up her hands in defeat. "Oh, go inside and find my housekeeper. Tell her that I said she is to give each of you a bath and feed you."

There was a loud cheer that utterly disturbed the peace of the garden.

"And mind your manners," Gideon warned with a look that promised dire retributions if he were not obeyed.

"Right, guv." The leader of the band of urchins offered a pert salute, then moving forward he eyed Gideon in a knowing manner. "The woman did disappear. I seen it."

"Unless you wish to be tossed out on your ear, I would suggest you forget what you think you might have seen," Gideon retorted in smooth tones.

There was a small pause before the lad gave a nod of his head. He was still young enough to accept that there were things in the world that could not be readily explained.

"Me memory has always given me trouble. A terrible thing it is," the boy retorted, offering Simone an awkward bow before hurrying after the other children into the house.

Turning, he met Simone's speaking glance.

"I do hope you realize my staff will be in mutiny by the end of the day," she informed him.

He gathered her in his arms. "What does it matter? We shall soon be wed and we shall have a new staff if we desire."

"Complete with six page boys?" she said wryly, although she willingly allowed herself to snuggle close to him.

"Six page boys, a vampire and the Guardian of the Medallion. It should be quite an interesting household," he teased, his hands stroking the satin of her hair.

She gave a small chuckle, her arms rising to wrap about his neck.

"As long as we are together."

He leaned downward to press his lips to her own.

"For eternity, my sweet."

Please turn the page for
an exciting sneak peek of
FEAR THE DARKNESS,
the next installment in Alexandra Ivy's
Guardians of Eternity series,
coming in September 2012!

Prologue
Sylvermyst Prophecy

Flesh of flesh, blood of blood, bound in darkness.
The Alpha and Omega shall be torn asunder
and through the mist reunited.
Pathways that have been hidden will be found
and the veil parted to the faithful.
The Gemini will rise and
chaos shall rule for all eternity.

Chapter 1

The abandoned silver mine in the Mojave Desert wasn't the first place one would expect to encounter Styx, the current Anasso.

Not only was he the King of all Vampires, but at six foot five of pure muscle with the stark beauty of his Aztec ancestors he was the one of the most powerful demons in the world.

He could command the most luxurious lair in the area with a dozen servants eager to do his bidding.

But he wanted his trip to Nevada to be as discreet as it was brief, so ignoring the protests of his companion, he'd chosen to spend the day waiting for his meeting with the local clan chief in the forgotten caves.

And, if he were honest with himself, it was a relief not to be stuck with the formal ceremony his position demanded. He was a fierce predator, not a damned politician, and the need to play nice gave him a rash.

Besides it was always a pleasure to yank Viper's chain.

Styx made a brief survey of the empty desert that surrounded them, absently knocking the dust from his leather pants that were tucked into a pair of heavy boots. A black T-shirt was stretched over his massive chest with a tiny amulet threaded on a leather strip wrapped around his thick neck. That was his only jewelry besides the polished turquoise stones that were threaded through the dark, braided hair that hung to the back of his knees.

His dark eyes glowed with power in the thickening dusk as he at last turned toward his companion, barely hiding his smile.

Unlike him, Viper, the clan chief of Chicago, had no love for 'roughing it.'

Dressed in a black velvet coat that reached his knees with a frilled white satin shirt and black slacks, he looked like he was on his way to the nearest ballroom. An impression only emphasized by his long hair the pale silver of moonlight that was left free to flow down his back and his eyes the startling darkness of midnight.

Styx was raw, savage power.

Viper was an exquisite fallen angel who was no less lethal.

With a pointed glance toward the Las Vegas skyline that glowed like a distant jewel, Viper met Styx's gaze with a sour grimace.

"The next time you want me to join you on a road trip, Styx, feel free to lose my number."

Styx arched a dark brow. "I thought everyone loved Vegas?"

"Which was why I agreed to this little excursion." Viper tugged at his lace cuffs, managing to look immaculate despite his hours in the dusty cavern. "You failed to mention I was going to be staying in a damned mine instead of the penthouse suite at the Bellagio."

"We've stayed in worse places."

"Worse?" Viper pointed a slender finger toward the rotting boards that did a half-ass job of covering the entrance to the tunnel. "It was filthy, it smelled of bat shit, and the temperature was a few degrees less than the surface of the sun. I've visited hell dimensions that I enjoyed more than that godforsaken inferno."

Styx snorted. The two vampires had been friends for centuries, a remarkable feat considering they were both alphas. But over the past months their bonds had grown even closer as they'd been forced to confront the increasingly dangerous world.

The Dark Lord (or Dark Prince or Master or a hundred other names he'd been called over the centuries) had been effectively banished from this dimension long ago and kept in his prison by the Phoenix, a powerful spirit who was being protected by the vampires. But he refused to take his imprisonment gracefully.

Over the past months he'd become increasingly relentless in his pursuit of smashing through the veils that separated the worlds, not only allowing his return, but giving a free pass to every creature that inhabited the numerous hells.

Only a few days ago the bastard had nearly succeeded.

Using one of the twin babies he'd created to use as a vessel for his grand resurrection, he'd transformed from a formless mist into a young, human-like female. It had been creepy as hell to see the ultimate of all evil looking like a pretty cheerleader.

And even creepier when he (or temporarily she) nearly crashed through the barrier to destroy them all.

Jaelyn (a fellow vampire) had managed to drain the Dark Lord before he could pass through the veil, but Styx knew it was only a temporary reprieve.

Until the Dark Lord was somehow destroyed, there would be no peace.

Which was why he was standing in the middle of the desert with a pissed-off Viper instead of waking in the arms of his beautiful mate.

"You're becoming as soft as a dew fairy in your old age," he mocked.

"I didn't become clan chief to rut in the dirt like some animal."

"Pathetic."

Viper glanced toward the distant glow of lights. "Are you at least going to tell me why we couldn't stay in one of the hundreds of hotels just a few miles away?"

Styx turned to scan the seemingly empty landscape.

Not that it was truly empty. At his feet a lizard crawled over a rock oblivious to the owl hunting in silence overhead, or the snake that was coiled only a few feet away. More distantly a coyote was on the trail of a jackrabbit.

The typical sights and sounds of the desert. His only interest, however, was making sure there were no nasty surprises hidden in the shadows.

"I prefer not to attract unwanted attention to our presence in Nevada," he explained. "Something that would be impossible with you in a casino."

"All I want is a warm shower, fresh clothes, and a ticket to the Donnie and Marie show."

"Do I have stupid tattooed on my forehead?" Styx turned to stab his friend with a knowing gaze. "The last time you were in Vegas you nearly bankrupted the Flamingo and ended up banned from returning to the city by the clan chief."

A reminiscent smile tugged at Viper's lips. "Can I help it if I happen to have a streak of luck at the craps table? Or that Roke is a humorless prig?"

The distant hum of a motorcycle sliced through the thick night air.

"Speaking of Roke," he murmured.

Viper muttered a curse as he moved to stand at Styx's side. "That's who we're meeting with?"

"Yes." Styx narrowed his gaze. "Do you promise to behave?"

"No, but I promise I won't kill him unless he . . ."

"Viper."

"Shit." Viper folded his arms over his chest. "This had better be important."

"Would I have left Darcy if it weren't?" he demanded, the mere mention of his mate sending a tiny pang of longing through his heart. Over the past months the beautiful female Were had become his very reason for living.

With a throaty roar of power, Roke brought his Turbine to a halt. Then, sliding off the elegant machine, he crossed to stand in front of them.

Dressed in black jeans, a leather jacket and moccasin boots that reached his knees, he was not as tall as Styx, although they shared the same bronzed skin and dark hair. Roke's, however, had been cut to brush his broad shoulders. His features were lean with the high cheekbones of his Native American bloodlines and a proud nose. His brow was wide and his lips generously full. But it was his eyes that captured and held attention.

Silver in color they were so pale they appeared almost white, the shocking paleness emphasized by the rim of pure black that circled them.

They were eyes that seemed to pierce through a person to lay bare their very souls.

Not always the most comfortable sensation.

Especially for those who didn't particularly want their souls laid bare.

Which was . . . yeah, pretty much everyone.

"Styx." Offering a low bow, Roke's movements were liquid smooth as he slowly straightened and with stunning swiftness was hurling a dagger to stick in the ground not an inch from Viper's expensive leather shoes. "Viper."

Viper growled, giving a wave of his hand to dislodge the dirt around Roke's feet. All vampires could manipulate the soil, a necessary skill to protect them from the sun or to hide the corpses of their prey, but Viper was particularly skilled and in less than a blink of an eye Roke was buried up to his waist.

"Are you two done playing?" Styx demanded, his icy power biting through the air.

The clan chief of Nevada climbed out of the sand pit and dusted off his jeans, his expression as inscrutable as ever.

"For now."

Viper made a sound of impatience. "Why are we here?"

Styx nodded toward their companion. "Roke has something he believes we should see."

"His collection of blow-up dolls?"

"Christ. Enough." Styx bared his massive fangs in warning. He didn't know what the hell had gone down between the two clan chiefs in the past, but right now he could not care less. He didn't have time for their bullshit. "Roke, show me."

"This way."

In utter silence the three vampires ghosted through

the darkness, moving with a speed that made them all but invisible. They were nearing a line of rugged hills when Viper made a sound of impatience.

"As much as I adore running through the barren desert, do we have an eventual destination?" he muttered.

On cue Roke came to a sharp halt, pointing toward the desert floor just in front of them.

"There."

Viper rolled his eyes. "Man of few words."

"Preferable to one who doesn't know when to shut it."

"Agreed," Styx said dryly, shifting so he could study the ground where Roke was pointing. It took a long moment to recognize that lines etched into the dry dirt were more than just the graffiti from some human. "Oh . . . shit."

"What the hell?" Viper tilted back his head as he caught the lingering scent. "Were."

"Cassandra," Styx said, easily recognizing the scent of his mate's twin sister who had recently been revealed as a powerful prophet.

"And Caine," Viper added. "Why would they be in the middle of the Mojave Desert?"

Now that was a hell of a question.

The pair of pureblooded Weres had been missing for weeks, despite Styx's best efforts to locate them. An unbelievable feat considering he possessed the best trackers in the world. Of course, if the rumors were true then the two Weres were already beyond his reach.

It made any clue as to how Cassandra had been captured, or how to retrieve her from her current prison priceless.

"I'm more concerned with what they left behind," he admitted, prowling around the edges of the strange symbols.

Viper frowned. "An etching?"

Styx shook his head. "It looks more like a hieroglyph."

"A prophecy," Roke said with a quiet confidence.

Styx turned to study the clan chief with a searching gaze. "Can you decipher it?"

"Yes, it's a warning."

Viper frowned. "You're a seer?"

Roke shook his head, his gaze trained on the lines etched into the ground.

"There's only one prophet. But I was sired by a wise woman who taught me to read the signs left by our forefathers."

Of course. Styx abruptly understood precisely why he was standing in the middle of a desert.

"So now we know why Cassandra chose to travel to Nevada," he said wryly.

"Why?" Viper demanded.

He pointed toward Roke. "Because it was the one place to make certain her message would be understood."

Viper snorted. "She could have sent a text and saved us a trip."

Styx's attention never wavered from the silent Roke.

It was impossible to judge how the vampire felt about being pulled into the battle against the Dark Lord.

But then, he no doubt realized that it wasn't a choice.

Styx wasn't the head of a damned democracy.

He led his people by cunning and brute force when necessary.

"How did you discover this?"

"A cur stumbled across it two nights ago," Roke promptly answered. "There are no Were packs in the area so he came to me with the information."

"How many others did he tell?"

Roke instantly understood Styx's concern. "None, but it's been here at least two, maybe even three weeks." He grimaced. "It's impossible to know how many others have seen it."

A pity, but there was nothing to be done, Styx silently conceded.

"Could anyone else interpret it?"

Roke paused before giving a shake of his head. "Doubtful."

Viper crouched down, studying the desert floor with a frown. "What does it say?"

Roke moved forward, careful not to disturb the marks as he pointed toward the strange etching closest to them. "This is the symbol for the Alpha and the Omega."

Styx froze at the familiar words.

"The children," he murmured, speaking of the twin babies that had been found by the half-Jinn mongrel,

Laylah. She hadn't known that they were the babies mentioned in the prophecies. Or that they had been created by the Dark Lord so he could use them as vessels for his eventual resurrection. "What about them?"

Roke traced the symbol in the air. "Here they are joined."

Styx nodded. When Laylah had found the children they'd been wrapped in the same stasis spell and she'd assumed there was only one child.

"Yes."

"And then they were separated." Roke pointed toward the second etching. "The Omega is lost to the mists."

Viper muttered a low curse. Styx didn't blame him.

They'd struggled to protect the children, but while Laylah and Tane had managed to rescue the boy child and name him Maluhia, the girl child had been taken through the barriers between dimensions and used by the Dark Lord in his attempt to return to this world.

Styx shifted his attention to the last symbol. "What's this?"

"The children reunited."

Hissing in disbelief, Styx turned to meet Roke's steady gaze, the pale silver eyes even more eerie than usual.

"Reunited?"

"'The Alpha and Omega shall be torn asunder and through the mists reunited,'" the clan chief of Nevada murmured, quoting the Sylvermyst Prophecy.

"Maluhia," Viper breathed, his expression grim. "Cassandra was warning us that the baby is in danger."

"Shit." Styx shoved his hand in his pocket to yank out his cell phone, his sense of furious urgency frustrated by the realization there was no service. He needed to get back to civilization. Now. Grasping the startled Roke by the upper arm, he headed back across the desert at a blinding speed. "You're coming with us."

Three weeks earlier
Las Vegas

The Forum shops in Caesar's Palace were a wonderland for any female, let alone one who had spent the past thirty years secluded from the world.

Beneath the ceilings that were painted to resemble a blue sky, the elegant stores wound their way past fountains that were intended to give the image of being transported back to Roman days, their glass display cases filled with the sort of temptation designed to make any woman drool.

With a wry smile, Caine stepped behind his dazzled companion to wrap his arms around her waist, tugging her back flat against his chest.

He could only wish Cassie would look at him with that same wistful longing, he ruefully acknowledged.

Or perhaps not, he swiftly corrected as his body hardened with a familiar, brutal need.

Since discovering Cassie being held prisoner in the cave of a demon lord weeks ago, Caine had done his best to play the role of Knight in Shining Armor.

After all, Cassie had not only been altered in the womb not to shift, but she was as innocent as a babe and twice as vulnerable.

Add in the fact she was the first true prophet born in centuries, and currently being hunted by every demon loyal to the Dark Lord, and she was a disaster waiting to happen.

She desperately needed a protector.

And since Caine (once a mere cur) had died and been resurrected as a pureblooded Were in her arms, he'd assumed that protecting Cassie was the reason the fates had returned him to this world instead of leaving him to rot in his well-deserved hell.

Unfortunately, his miraculous return to life hadn't included a sainthood and he remained a fully, functioning male with all the usual weaknesses.

Including a rampaging lust toward the tiny female currently wrapped in his arms.

As always completely impervious to his torment, Cassie breathed a soft sigh of wonder.

"Oh . . ."

"Cassie." Bending down, he spoke directly in her ear. "Cassie, listen to me."

She tilted back her head to meet his narrowed gaze and Caine briefly forgot how to breathe.

Holy shit, but she was beautiful.

Her hair was pale, closer to silver than blond, and pulled into a ponytail that fell to her waist. Her skin was a perfect alabaster, smooth and silken. Her eyes were an astonishing green, the color of spring grass and flecked with gold.

Her face was heart-shaped with delicate features that gave her an air of fragility that was only emphasized by her slender body. Of course, beneath her jeans and casual sweatshirt, she possessed the lean muscles of all pure-blooded Weres.

"What?" she prompted when he continued to gawk at her in mindless appreciation.

He sucked in a deep breath, savoring the warm scent of lavender that clung to her skin.

"You promised me that you would blend."

She wiggled from his grasp and darted toward the nearest store to press her face against the window.

"Mmmm. Pretty."

Caine rolled his eyes. "I knew this was a mistake."

"There's so many," she murmured as he moved to stand beside her. "How do you choose?"

"We'll go into a store, pick out a few of your favorite clothes, and try them on . . ."

"Okay."

Without waiting for him finish, Cassie was darting through the open doorway. Caine was swiftly on her heels, but with immaculate timing a buxom nymph with dark hair and brown eyes pretended to stumble and landed against his chest.

Instinctively his hands reached to grasp her shoulders, his sapphire blue eyes narrowed with irritation.

Once upon a time he had appreciated beautiful females tossing themselves into his arms. Even though he'd been a mere cur, his short blond hair that fell across his brow and tanned, surfer good-looks made sure he had more than his fair share of babes. And it didn't hurt that his body was chiseled with lean muscles beneath the low-riding jeans and tight T-shirt.

And oh yeah, he'd made an obscene fortune cranking out prescription drugs from his private lab.

Now it took every ounce of willpower to politely set aside the damned nymph and not toss her into the line of sleek metallic mannequins showing off the latest designer swimwear.

"Didn't we meet in . . ." she began, but Caine wasn't listening as he swept past her and headed straight toward the tiny blonde who was fingering a white sundress with black polka dots.

"Cassie."

He had barely reached her side when her hands reached for the bottom of her sweatshirt and began pulling it over her head.

"I want to try it on."

"Holy shit." He grabbed her hands, yanking the sweatshirt back into place. "Wait."

She frowned in confusion. “But you said . . .”

“Yeah, I know what I said,” he muttered. When was he going to learn she took every word quite literally?

“Did I do something wrong?”

“Never.” He brushed a finger over her pale cheek. Christ, she was so unbearably innocent. “Why don’t you show me what you like and I’ll pick out the right size?”

“You can do that just by looking?”

His lips twisted in a dry smile. “It’s a gift.”

“A well-practiced gift?”

He stilled, regarding her in surprise. Despite the fact they’d been constant companions over the past weeks, Cassie rarely seemed aware of his presence, let alone the fact that he was a red-blooded male.

Not that he took it personally.

She was plagued by her visions of the future and too often impervious to the world around her.

“Are you truly interested?” he husked.

She flashed him a dimpled smile. “Perhaps.”

He swallowed a growl, his body once again hard and aching. She was going have him a raving lunatic before this was over.

“Better than nothing.” He motioned toward the hovering saleslady, indicating he wanted one of the sundresses before steering Cassie toward the khaki shorts and pretty summer tops. “Now, let’s choose a few sensible outfits before we move on.”

Within an hour they had a reasonable pile of clothes

for both of them and a bill that would make most men shudder in horror.

Caine, however, didn't so much as flinch as he gathered the packages and headed out of the store. They had left Missouri after Cassie had offered her warning to Laylah with nothing more than the clothes on their backs. Tonight he intended to enjoy a hot shower, clean clothes, good food, and a soft bed.

In that order.

In silence they wandered down the wide passageway, occasionally halting for Cassie to peer into the windows.

For the moment Caine was content to allow her to behave as a normal female. It was all too rare that she was able to put aside the burden of her visions.

And as long as he didn't detect any danger lurking . . .

His brain closed down as his searching gaze was snared by the sight of lace and ribbons and feminine temptation spread in front of a shop window.

Instinct alone had him herding Cassie through the door and into the hushed atmosphere of the exclusive store.

"What are you doing?" she asked in confusion.

"We did your shopping, now it's my turn," he informed her, moving toward a table that held a pile of satin teddies.

Oh . . . hell.

Cassie halted at his side, her expression puzzled. "Here?"

"Absolutely." Dropping his packages, Caine reached

for a scarlet teddie, holding up the fragile garment for her inspection. "What do you think?"

"Tiny." There was a faint hint of dimples. "I don't think it will fit you."

Heat blasted through him at the vivid image of Cassie wearing the lacy lingerie and spread across his bed, that same almost-smile teasing at her lips.

"We'll take one of each color," he croaked toward the saleswoman.

"They're not very practical," she protested.

"Practical is the last thing you should be when you're wearing fine lingerie."

Expecting an argument, Caine was caught off-guard when she reached to gently stroke a finger over the shimmering fabric.

"I suppose they'll be comfortable to sleep in."

Sleep?

Caine's fantasy abruptly altered to reality. Which meant Cassie sleeping like a baby in one bed while he tossed and turned in another.

Did he really need to add in a skimpy bit of silk to increase torture?

"For one of us," he wryly admitted.

Predictably she didn't have a clue why he was suddenly questioning his own sanity.

"What?"

He headed toward the discreet sales desk at the back of the store, pulling his wallet from his pocket.

"I'm an idiot."

Please turn the page for
an exciting sneak peek of
MY LORD ETERNITY,
the next installment in Alexandra Ivy's
Immortal Rogues series,
coming in December 2012!

Chapter I

Although Miss Jocelyn Kingly had never before encountered the devil, she was fairly certain he was currently sitting in her front parlor.

It was not so much his appearance that made her think of the Lord of the Netherworld, she grudgingly conceded.

Indeed, he might have been a beloved angel with his long, tawny curls that framed a lean countenance and brushed his wide shoulders. His eyes were a pure, shimmering gold with long black lashes that would make any woman gnash her teeth in envy. His features were carved with a delicate male beauty.

But there was nothing angelic in the decided glint of wicked humor in those magnificent eyes and sensuous cut of those full lips.

And, of course, the indecent charm of those deep dimples.

She should have sent him on his way the moment he arrived upon her doorstep. Not even for a moment should she be considering the notion of allowing such a disturbing gentleman into her home.

She would have to be mad.

When she had first been struck with the notion of renting her attics, it had been with the prospect of discovering a quiet, comfortable tenant. Someone who would not disturb the peace of her household.

Unfortunately there were few such tenants who desired to live in a neighborhood that hovered on the edge of the stews. The local pickpockets and prostitutes did not possess the funds to pay the rent, even if she were to consider allowing them into her home. And the few gentlemen who possessed businesses in the area already owned their own property, usually far from St. Giles.

Which left Lucien Valin.

A shiver raced down her spine.

If only she were not in such desperate need of money.

If only it were not a full two months until her quarterly allowance.

If only . . .

Her lips twitched with wry humor. She could devote the next fortnight to listing the "if-onlys" in her life. Now was not the time for such futile longings.

She better than anyone understood that the mistakes of the past could not be altered. One could only ensure that they were not repeated.

Unconsciously straightening her spine Jocelyn forced herself to meet that piercing golden gaze. It came as no surprise to discover her visitor's lips were twitching as if he were amused by her obvious hesitation.

"So, Miss Kingly, was the newspaper in error?" he prodded in that husky, faintly accented voice. "Do you have rooms to let or not?"

The voice of a devil. Jocelyn sucked in a steadying breath. Devil or not, he was the only potential tenant who offered the cold, hard coin she so desperately needed.

There had to be something said for that. Unfortunately.

"There are rooms," she agreed in cautious tones. "However, I feel it incumbent to warn you that they are located in the garret and are quite cramped. I am uncertain that a gentleman of your large proportions would find them at all comfortable."

His slender, powerful hands moved to steeple beneath his chin, the golden eyes shimmering in the slanting morning sunlight.

"Do not fear, I am tall, but thankfully, quite intelligent. I need hit my head upon the rafters on only a handful of occasions to recall to duck."

"There is also our unfortunate proximity to the slaughterhouses. The stench can be unbearable on some days."

"I have discovered that there are few places in London that are not plagued with one unpleasant odor or another. Not even Mayfair is unaffected."

Jocelyn maintained her calm demeanor with an effort. She never allowed herself to be ruffled. She had learned through painful experience that to lose control was a certain invitation to disaster.

"Unlike Mayfair, however, this neighborhood can be quite dangerous as well."

His dimples suddenly flashed. "Surely, my dear, you do not suppose Mayfair to be without its dangers? Just imagine . . . marriage-mad mamas, overdressed fops fragrant with the stench of rosewater, and a prince who insists upon keeping his chambers as smothering hot as the netherworld. It is enough to terrify the stoutest of hearts." He lifted one broad shoulder. "I should be able to hold my own against a handful of thieves and street urchins."

There was no reasonable argument to refute his confident words. Although he cloaked himself in a lazy charm, there was no mistaking the fluid power of his male form or the hint of ruthless will that was etched upon the lean features.

Only a fool would underestimate the danger of Mr. Lucien Valin. And Jocelyn was no fool.

"If you say," she reluctantly conceded.

"Is there anything else?"

"There are my rules, of course," she swiftly countered, not at all surprised when his lips curled in open amusement.

"Of course."

"This is not a lodging house. I live very quietly. I will not countenance loud gatherings or drunken carousing."

A tawny brow flicked upward. "I am allowed no callers?"

"Only if they are discreet."

For some reason her cool response only deepened his amusement. "Ah."

That unwelcome shiver once again inched down her spine, and Jocelyn discovered herself battling back the words to order this Mr. Valin from her house.

She did not have the luxury of turning away a perfectly suitable tenant just because of some vague fear.

"And the arrangement will be of a temporary nature," she instead retorted in an effort to reassure her faltering nerve. "No longer than two months."

"That suits me well enough."

It appeared everything suited the devil.

Jocelyn narrowed her gaze. "I also must insist that you respect my privacy. You are welcome to eat in the kitchen with Meg, but the remainder of the house is not to be entered."

There was a brief pause as he studied her carefully bland countenance. Then he gave a vague nod of his head. "As you wish. Is that all?"

It was, of course.

She was charging him an outrageous sum of money for cramped rooms and meals he would be forced to eat in the servants' quarters.

She had also made impossible rules that would annoy the most even-tempered of gentlemen.

The mere fact that he had so readily agreed made her even more suspicious.

"Why are you here?" she demanded in abrupt tones.

His hands lowered as he regarded her with a bemused smile.

"I beg your pardon?"

Jocelyn deliberately allowed her gaze to drop to the deep burgundy coat cut by an obvious expert and white waistcoat stitched with silver thread. Her gaze continued over the hard, muscular thrust of his legs to linger upon the glossy Hessians that cost more than many families could earn in a year.

At last she raised her head to discover him regarding her in a curious fashion. "It is obvious that you are a gentleman of means, Mr. Valin. Why would you desire to take inferior rooms in a neighborhood most consider fit only for cutthroats and whores?"

"Does it truly matter what my reason?" he demanded softly.

"I will not harbor a criminal."

He gave a sudden chuckle. "I assure you that I am not hiding from the gallows."

"Then, why?"

"Let us just say that there was a slight misunderstanding with my cousin."

The explanation was a trifle too smooth for her liking.

"You had a slight misunderstanding with your cousin

and now you desire to hide in St. Giles? You shall have to do better than that, Mr. Valin."

The devilish glint in the golden eyes became even more pronounced. "Perhaps it was more than a slight misunderstanding. Gideon can unfortunately be tiresomely unreasonable when he chooses, and I believe there was some mention of a nasty duel. It seemed best to avoid him for the next several weeks. Just until his temper is recovered."

"What is the nature of this misunderstanding?"

His features unexpectedly firmed to uncompromising lines. "That is a private matter."

A woman, Jocelyn silently concluded, caught off guard by a traitorous prick of disappointment.

What else could she expect from such a gentleman? He was, after all, born to break the heart of susceptible women.

Then she was severely chastising herself for her unworthy thoughts.

She knew nothing of this gentleman. Certainly not enough to brand him as a womanizing letch. And in truth, even if he were, she was in no position to judge another.

"I respect your privacy, but you must understand that I have no desire to discover an angry gentleman upon my doorstep with his dueling pistol."

The incorrigible humor swiftly returned to the bronze features. "He has no means of discovering I am here. Besides, Gideon would never harm a lady. He far prefers to charm them." His smile became decidedly suggestive. "As do I."

Jocelyn carefully laid her hands upon her tidy desk. This flirtatious banter was precisely what she had feared from Mr. Valin. It was important that she put a swift end to any hopes he might harbor of a casual seduction.

"That is all very well, but do not imagine for a moment, Mr. Valin, that I am remotely interested in any charms you might claim to possess."

Far from wounded by her firm words, the gentleman stroked a slender finger down the length of his jaw.

"Surely you exaggerate, Miss Kingly? Not even remotely interested?"

"No."

He heaved a teasing sigh. "A hard woman."

"A sensible woman who has no time for foolish games," she corrected him firmly. "You would do well to remember my warning."

"Oh, I possess a most excellent memory," he drawled, reaching beneath his jacket to remove a small leather bag that he placed upon the desk. "Indeed, I even remembered this."

She eyed the bag warily. "What is it?"

"The two months' rent in advance, just as you requested."

Jocelyn made no effort to reach for the money. She knew the moment her fingers touched the coins she would be irrevocably committed to allowing this gentleman into her home.

And yet, what else could she do?

There was nothing particularly noble in bare cupboards and empty coal bins. And besides, she had Meg to consider.

Her old nurse was the only one to stand beside her when the scandal had broken. She was the only friend she had left in the world.

How could she possibly allow the older woman to suffer even further hardship?

The answer, of course, was she could not. This money would pay their most pressing creditors and put food on the table. At the moment that was all that mattered.

Grimly thrusting aside the warning voice that whispered in the back of her mind, Jocelyn gave a nod of her head.

"Thank you."

As if thoroughly aware of her inner struggle, the devil lifted his brows in a faintly mocking manner.

"Do you not wish to count it?"

"That will not be necessary."

"So trusting, my dove?"

"You will not be difficult to track down if I discover you have attempted to cheat me."

"There is that," he agreed with a chuckle. "When may I take possession of the rooms?"

Although not always meticulously devoted to truth if

a small bit of subterfuge was more practical, Jocelyn discovered herself unable to form the lie that would allow her a few days' grace from Mr. Valin's presence.

Not that it truly mattered.

She would no doubt merely waste the days brooding upon what was to come. Surely this was like swallowing vile medicine. It was best to be done with quickly.

"The rooms have been cleaned and prepared," she forced herself to admit. "You may have them whenever you desire."

"Good. I will collect my belongings and be here later this afternoon."

This afternoon.

She absolutely refused to shiver again.

"What of your cousin?" she demanded. "Will he not shoot you when you return for your belongings?"

"I have it on excellent authority that he devoted the goodly portion of the evening to his current mistress. It will be several hours before he awakens."

She unconsciously grimaced. "I see."

An odd hint of satisfaction touched the handsome countenance. "You disapprove of such pleasurable pastimes, Miss Kingly?"

Jocelyn was swift to smooth her features to calm indifference. "I do not possess sufficient interest to disapprove, Mr. Valin."

His lips twisted wryly. "No, of course not."

Having strained her nerves quite far enough for one morning, Jocelyn rose to her feet.

"I believe we have covered everything, Mr. Valin."

Efficiently dismissed, the tawny-haired gentleman reluctantly pushed himself from his chair.

"I shall return in a few hours," he was swift to warn.

Jocelyn, however, was prepared on this occasion.

"If you have need of anything, please speak with Meg. She is quite capable and is in full control of the household."

The golden eyes narrowed as she easily maneuvered him firmly into the hands of her servant.

"More capable than you, Miss Kingly?" he demanded in those husky tones.

"Without a doubt." With a crisp nod of her head she regained her seat and reached for her ledger book. "Good-bye, Mr. Valin."

He remained standing beside the desk, but as she kept her gaze upon the pages of her accounts, he at last gave a low chuckle.

"Until later, my dear."

Jocelyn maintained her charade of distraction until she at last heard the sound of the door closing behind his retreating form. Only then did she lean back in her seat and close her eyes in an odd weariness.

There would be dinner on the table tonight.

But what was the cost?

And was she prepared to pay it?